Into the

Abyss

Vault of Verona

Marissa Price

The Literature Factory
Publishing Division
Hudson Way, Ningi
Queensland, Australia 4511

www.theliteraturefactory.com.au

This paperback edition published 2017

Published by The Literature Factory, 2017

This novel is entirely a work of fiction, based on the original play of William Shakespeare titled 'Romeo and Juliet'. The names, characters and incidents portrayed in it are the work of the author's imagination, with the exception of the aforementioned links with William Shakespeare's original play. Any resemblance to actual persons, living or dead or events is entirely coincidental.

A catalogue record for this book is available at the State Library of Queensland

Paperback ISBN 978-0-6481279-0-1
eBook ISBN 978-0-6481279-1-8
Hardcover ISBN 978-0-6481279-4-9

Printed in Australia by IngramSpark

*For my family
Glenn, Cayla and Cameron*

Into the Abyss

Vault of Verona

Chapter One

Harriet Hunter threw herself down onto her bed, crushing the stray clothes and dog eared novels scattered across the blanket. Though the clothes overflowed from Harriet's dresser drawers onto the timber floorboards of her room, her collection of soccer and dancing medals from years past stood neatly in rows on the shelves of her desk. Everything had a place in Harriet's world, it just wasn't always in it.

She sighed loudly as she yanked a folded sheet of paper from the backpack tossed haphazardly beside the bed. Another English assignment. It felt like just yesterday that Harriet had finished an English exam: how could it possibly be time for another? Scowling, Harriet rolled over and concentrated on reading the instructions at the top of the paper. Romeo and Juliet. Great. If ever there was a story where women were meek, mild and boring, this was it. Who stabs themselves in the heart just because some guy with a fancy hairdo and a cape drank some poison? Honestly.

Harriet humphed as she flipped over to the criteria page, scowling as she hunted for the word count. Rewrite part of Shakespeare's play using an example Mrs Wellington had not covered in class, in 600 words or less. No problem.

Harriet was an exceptional writer. She sat up, just a little bit brighter that her whole weekend wasn't lost, and eased her laptop out of the computer bag. She briefly considered what her mother would say if she could see her now. There would be plenty about how much her desk had cost, and how slouching causes bad posture. But the bed was just so much more inviting. Settling herself comfortably with her back to the head board, Harriet tapped 'Harrypotter' into the password box and hit enter, her tongue between her teeth. Snatching up a pencil from the bedside table, Harriet tapped the criteria page, searching for a story option that caught her interest.

"Hmmm…nope," Harriet muttered to herself, as she crossed out the option of Juliet marrying Paris. "Boring".

Harriet scanned down the page, rejecting suggestion after suggestion until she was out of ideas. None of the predefined concepts caught her interest, or inspired her to begin writing. She considered the last option, an open invitation to fracture the story in some way. She tapped her pencil against her computer as her brain whirred, sifting through the character types they had read in class. She certainly didn't want to write about a meek Juliet, or about a Romeo whom she had perceived as a spoilt young man with a thirst for violence. Harriet was much more interested in strong women, people like Emma Watson who stood up for what they believed in. But Emma was a modern woman, and she had to deal with one stuck back in the middle ages.

Harriet's brain snapped into focus like the last line falling into place on a Rubix cube. There was no reason why she couldn't change the characters to make them more modern…she could create an interesting, dynamic Juliet who wouldn't back down from a fight with anyone. *Make Juliet's character into a modern woman,* Harriet mused. Interesting. This might just do. Harriet slapped a piece of scrap paper on the lid of her laptop and sketched a few quick ideas. She drew a passable sketch of Juliet's face, although something looked a little wonky or lopsided, like most of Harriet's attempts at art. The face that emerged wasn't the face of

Olivia Hussey in the 1968 film version they'd watched in class. Nor was it the image of Claire Danes, who'd acted alongside Leo and worn those feathered wing things. It was a strong face that appeared – it was the image of a woman who knew what she wanted. A firm chin, mobile mouth and spirited eyes stared back from the paper at Harriet. Long brown hair, fierce brows and high cheekbones completed the drawing. Harriet pursed her lips as she shaded in the last of the hair, and tilted her head as she scribbled. Unwittingly, she had created an image that melded elements of what looked like her own face with those she imagined Juliet possessed. Or would have possessed anyway, if she'd had a spine of her own and had stood up to the myriad of people who wanted to run her life for her.

Harriet wouldn't consider herself a feminist. Not in the way that traditional feminists were viewed anyway. She thought of herself as more of an equalist, if there was such a thing. Men and women, navigating the world together on terms that suited them individually. She'd never understood why girls couldn't play soccer, or boys couldn't dance ballet. She'd done both, and although she hadn't been the best at either one, she'd had fun.

There had been something about the story of Romeo and Juliet that had irked Harriet as the class worked their way through the laborious Shakespearean text. More, it had rankled that the other girls in her class had seemed unconcerned about how Juliet was portrayed. They didn't see anything unusual or wrong in Juliet's actions and choices, or the way she meekly accepted the edicts of the men around her. Even her ultimate act of impassioned suicide was spurred on by the loss of a man. Sure, Romeo was a pretty good catch, all things considered. But whether it's really worth dying for the lost love of another was a bit of a stretch. And there had to be a better way to get out of marrying Paris than pretending to kill yourself. Such a risky endeavour, especially in medieval Italy.

Harriet's classmates had snickered when she'd offered her thoughts on that matter. She could still see Gracie Finkle smirking at her from between two of the most popular boys in the grade. They were boys who would never look twice at Harriet. She knew it, and so did Gracie Finkle. Harriet constantly told herself that she didn't care anyway, they were boys and they were gross. But there was a little part of Harriet that was starting to care, and it irritated her.

Harriet was jolted from her reverie by her father's voice booming up the stairway towards her bedroom. Dinner was ready, and she was expected, pronto. Harriet tucked the drawing into the side of her folded laptop, threw the computer carelessly on the bed and headed downstairs for dinner. Logan Hunter was standing in the kitchen, portioning out mashed vegetables and pork chops. Harriet swiped a finger through the steaming mashed potatoes as her father turned back to put the frying pan on the stove.

"I saw that."

Harriet smiled cheekily, as Logan turned and raised an eyebrow at her.

In the distance, Harriet heard the front door slam shut and the jingle of her mother's keys.

"I'm home," she called out, appearing around the corner and into the dining room. She was balancing mountains of paperwork, a laptop and a handbag in her arms. Logan rushed to help his wife unload her bags as Harriet scooped up the silverware from the kitchen counter.

"Where are the monsters?" Harriet asked, registering the unusual quiet in the lower level of the house. Her question was answered by the whooping of her two brothers who had spied their mother from outside. They came rushing in from the sunny backyard, still light but with the lengthening shadows of a long summer. Carolyn Hunter kissed her boys on the cheek as they danced around her, each one as filthy as the next. She laughed.

"Wash your hands, boys," she said, kissing her husband's cheek as well. She ran her hand over Harriet's long brown hair as she walked past, setting the table for dinner.

Logan returned to the kitchen and finished dishing out the peas.

"What did you do today, Harriet?" he asked, deftly catching a stray pea as it tried to escape from one of the plates.

"Nothing, really," Harriet said in a non-committal tone. Logan exchanged a look with his wife over Harriet's head. Carolyn shook hers.

"Surely you did something, sweetie!" Carolyn said in a bright voice. Harriet didn't respond. They'd had this argument before, and she wasn't looking to get into it again. Last time she'd almost been forced to join the school netball team. Harriet shuddered.

"I have an English assignment to do," Harriet said, trying to distract her parents. "I have to rewrite Romeo and Juliet in some other way. I thought about making Juliet a little more modern, and a little less of a door mat."

Carolyn pursed her lips. She glanced at Logan before she answered. "That sounds like a great idea," she said, watching her husband's reaction. He grunted.

"Never understood why he didn't check a little more thoroughly that she was dead in the first place," he said, transferring plates from the counter to the table. "But I don't remember the story very well; it's been a while since I was in high school."

Mason and Tristan tumbled back into the dining room, hands clean from scrubbing. They sat down in their chairs, chattering to each other like little monkeys. Harriet and her parents took their seats.

"You know," said Carolyn. "I never understood why you stopped playing soccer." So they weren't going to avoid this again.

"Wasn't interested," Harriet replied, through a mouthful of mashed potatoes.

"But...aren't you bored?" Carolyn asked, her brow wrinkled. "All you ever do is read books."

"That's not a bad thing, Carolyn," Logan replied in a mild tone. "I quite enjoy a good book myself."

"Yes honey," said Carolyn, a note of impatience in her tone. "But Harriet is a young lady, she should be out with her friends, shopping, playing netball, even dancing. What about looking into dancing again, Harriet?"

Logan sat silently, cutting his meat as Harriet made a production out of chewing her food.

"I don't really think I'd be any good at it now, Mum," Harriet said, finally. "I'm not stick thin, and all the girls my age are getting up on pointe shoes now. I'd be like a dancing elephant."

Logan frowned at the last comment. Carolyn blew out an exasperated breath.

"Well that's a little dramatic, don't you think? You're built well for dancing!"

"I have your thighs…isn't that what you always say? And you refuse to wear a swimsuit because of those thighs. I refuse to wear a leotard and prance around in tights and little else."

The boys were watching the exchange between Harriet and their mother, their heads whipping back and forth like spectators at a tennis match. Harriet's face was mulish and threatened a brewing storm, and Carolyn's wasn't far behind. They'd always clashed, ever since Harriet was a little girl. Her grandmother said it was because they were so similar, but Harriet thought she was more like her father.

"It wouldn't hurt to try something new, would it Harriet?" Logan said, sensing impending doom and desperately trying to avoid it.

Harriet had heard enough. She always felt like she wasn't enough, like she didn't do what was expected of her as her mother's daughter. She pushed back from the table.

"Thanks for dinner Dad," she said, her tone soft and a little shaky. "I'm going to go up to bed, I've had enough…to eat. May I please be excused?" It came out more as a demand than a question.

Logan sighed wearily and glanced at his wife. Carolyn remained silent, her eyes locked on her daughter's face.

"Go," Logan said, his tone softer than his words. Harriet knew that he tried to keep the peace, and felt sorry for her role in his need to do that. It was difficult to control her responses and she knew that another prod from her mother would send her temper soaring. Harriet deposited her plate on the bench and took the steps to her room two at a time. She swung her door shut behind her and flung herself down on her bed, face first. Screaming silently into the pillow, she let out the frustration that these encounters with her mother created in her. Both were strong women, and for that reason they clashed on a regular basis. It frustrated Harriet no end, and she felt as though she would never be good enough for her mother just as she was. Carolyn was a partner working at a top tier law firm, an important and powerful woman in her professional sphere. Harriet knew that her mother wanted that kind of success for her, but for now, Harriet just wanted to enjoy herself. She'd seen what it had taken for her mother to reach the top of the corporate ladder and she wasn't sure she wanted that kind of life for herself. She dreamt of writing – her own stories out there for other people to enjoy.

A tinkling *ding* from Harriet's bedside table caught her attention. She rolled her head to the side and opened one eye. She saw that a message had flashed up on the screen, and Harriet grabbed the phone and partly sat up to read it. It was from Tessa, Harriet's closest friend. Despite her mood, she grinned as she read Tessa's latest gripe about her boyfriend, Todd. Though Harriet was glad she didn't have to deal with the seemingly constant drama of having a boyfriend, she was a little envious at times of the dates Tessa went on with Todd. All of the girls in her grade seemed to be pairing off with the boys, though Harriet doubted that they all really liked each other. It was a status symbol to have a boyfriend, and the girls who didn't were looked at askance. Harriet felt the judgment as she walked to her locker alone, or as she moved between classes without someone hanging off her arm. It bothered her, but not enough for her to pretend that she liked any of the boys who had asked her out. Especially Gideon White. They'd been friends since the first grade, for goodness sake. There was no way that she'd view him as anything more than a brother, no matter how hard their friends pushed to get them together.

Harriet settled in for a fast paced text conversation and soon forgot about Gideon, the fight with her parents and the paper peeking out the side of her laptop. Even as she grew tired and settled down into her pillows, the assignment remained forgotten, obscured by talk of plans for trips to the beach on the school holidays. As Harriet's eyes grew heavy, she reached out instinctively to put her phone on the charger, then snuggled deeper into her pillows. Before long she was asleep, the Romeo and Juliet assignment left to another day.

Chapter Two

The storm that echoed the one in Harriet's heart flew through her open windows in the early hours of the morning. Usually at this time, the Tasmanian air was still, heavy and laden with the promise of a new day. But in the wee hours of this morning, the air was alive, kicked up by squally winds that made Harriet's curtains billow. Although the thunder rumbled and the lightening flashed, there was only a light rain that failed to pull Harriet from her deep sleep. She snuggled closer into the pillow and pulled the blankets up around her neck as the air cooled considerably.

There was a tinkling crash as one of Harriet's tiny tot ballet medals fell from a high shelf of her desk to the one below. The stormy air swirled through the room, making clothes hanging from the drawers flutter and sway. Harriet's drawing of her Juliet character was pulled and tugged by the swirling gales from its place in the closed laptop, finally popping out as a particularly strong wind gust rattled the windows and screens. It fluttered through the air, dancing with the wind, before settling next to Harriet's open hand. Her other hand was tucked under her face, cushioning her head. Harriet sensed the fluttering paper beside her, and through a haze of sleep she instinctively put a hand out to stop it from flying away. Drowsily, she tucked the sheet more securely under her arm, up near her face and the pillow.

Her dreams were particularly vivid tonight. Screaming horses and clashing swords; heavy, trailing gowns and billowing headdresses flashed behind her eyes. Harriet shifted restlessly in her sleep, the drawing crumpling slightly under her shoulder as she flipped over. As the wind died off and the curtains lay still again, Harriet, drifted down into a deep sleep, a frown on her face.

***

Harriet rose to the jaunty chirping of birds outside her window. She rolled over sleepily, trying to avoid the beam of sunshine that fell onto her face as the curtains shifted in the breeze. She felt unusually warm, quite hot even, and through her sleepy state Harriet registered confusion. Had her parents left the heating on, perhaps? She stretched lazily beneath the covers, knowing it was Saturday morning and unless she wanted to watch cartoons, there was little else she needed to rise for. A few hours with the Romeo and Juliet story writing and she'd be done. She just needed to go online to know a little more about what it was like living as a woman in Shakespeare's time before she could start planning.

Harriet sighed and rolled over, burying her head under the pillows, just as the door to her room crashed open and a foreign, heavily accented voice rang out.

"Juliet! It is morning, Juliet! And what a morning it is!" Harriet sat up abruptly in bed, disoriented and confused. She watched blearily as a heavy set woman in a plain, serviceable and, quite frankly, huge, gown bustled around the room. She winced as the woman swished the curtains back and deftly tied them. Then she stared at the heavy, embroidered drapes adorning the windows, instead of her white, sheer curtains. And the walls surrounding the windows! Gone were the white plastered walls with posters of her favourite bands and movies. In its place was a heavy, dark stone wall, the blocks huge and intimidating.

Harriet's eyes widened as her gaze swept around the room. She registered the huge four poster bed she was lying in, very different to her own serviceable double ensemble. Beginning to panic a little, Harriet realised she was no longer in her own room. The air was different here, heavier and warmer as she had felt before, and she was surrounded by things that were foreign to her. Her heart beat faster as sleep fully receded and she remembered there was still someone else in the room with her.

"Juliet!" Harriet jumped as the older woman barked the name. "What are you still doing abed! We must dress you and get you ready, today is not the day to dally! Come child! There are Lords and Ladies from all over the land arriving today. They'll all wish to see you before the wedding tomorrow."

Wait. Hold on. What now? Wedding? Harriet's mind scrambled. Where on earth WAS she?

"Ah there it is," the older lady crooned as she extracted a delicate, braided gold headband from the robe in the corner. She polished the band on her sleeve as she advanced on the bed. "This one has been in the Capulet family for generations. It's only fitting that you wear it today to greet your guests."

Capulet? Harriet's eyes popped wide open. She yanked the covers up and frantically searched for her drawing. For her laptop, for anything from a time she remembered. Her hands touched the crisp, white drawing paper as she skated them desperately under her mountain of pillows. Breathing a sigh of relief that at least something still remained as it had been before, she pulled the sheet out and glanced at it. It was identical to the drawing from the night before. The same face stared back at her, partially her own features mixed in with those of someone else.

"What have you got there?" the old lady asked as she stoked the fire in the corner. A large pitcher stood next to its cheery warmth, welcoming despite the heat of the day. "Come child, why so lazy today?" It took some labouring on Harriet's part to understand the words delivered in the thickly accented voice. Was that Italian? Her languages teacher at school didn't sound like that when she ran through numbers and colours in Italian class. Capulet. Italian. Juliet. Harriet's mind raced as she frantically recalled the characters in Romeo and Juliet. She couldn't remain mute forever, sooner or later she'd have to say something.

"Nurse?" Harriet asked, tentatively.

"Who else would I be? What's wrong with you, young lady?" Nurse demanded, her hands fisted on her hips and her face flushed pink. Her grey hair was starting to curl around her face from the heat and exertion. She blew a curl back from her eye and began to shift something heavy on the other side of an ornate screen standing in the corner of the room, near the fire. Nurse grunted as whatever it was screeched and groaned as it was wrestled into place.

Harriet's mind raced as she tried to wrap her head around what was happening. She shoved the drawing back under the pillow instinctively, wanting to keep her little piece of home safe. Reluctantly, she crawled out of bed and stood on the bare floor that was not her own. Gone were the warm timber floorboards underneath her bed. Instead, her feet had found cold stone, chilly despite the hot morning. Uncertainly, Harriet stood, her arms wrapped around herself. She watched as Nurse bent over to pick up a towel from behind the screen, her large bottom waving in the air.

"There. That ought to do it. Lord's mercy child, don't just stand there!" Nurse demanded as she turned around, puffing slightly. "Get in the tub!"

Harriet looked around for a bathtub from her own time. There was a large container that looked like a cauldron in the corner, mostly hidden by the screen. Nurse had been pushing and pulling that into place – this must be what she was referring to.

"Gown off!" Nurse demanded, as she turned around with a pail of water in her hands. That jolted Harriet from her dream state. She blinked at Nurse and her mind balked at the command. She didn't want to disrobe in front of a total stranger, and she crossed her arms over her chest protectively. Even though she knew Nurse's character from reading the story of Romeo and Juliet, she didn't understand how on earth she seemed to be *in* the story. It was a work of fiction, dreamed up by the mind of Shakespeare. It made no sense for Harriet to be here. Yet, her surroundings told her that she likely was, and Nurse's crossed arms and darkening expression suggested that her patience was running out. Harriet had to do something…she had to go along with this and see how it played out. She didn't see another option at this point in time.

"Come on my Lady, we don't have all day!" Exasperation and impatience rang in Nurse's voice.

Harriet wasn't yet ready to expose herself as a fraud, not until she knew if it was dangerous. Neither did she want to get undressed.

"I…I can do it myself, Nurse," Harriet said timidly.

"Of course you can't, my Lady!" Nurse said crossly. "This pitcher weighs more than you do. Now hop in and sit down. The Blessed Mother knows there isn't a freckle on your body I've not seen before, having nursed you since you were a babe. Hurry now." Nurse's arms were straining and her face was turning decidedly red. Harriet hurried to strip off her nightgown, staring at the rich embroidery on the long sleeves and the lace adorning much of the top half. These were certainly not her pyjamas, or the clothes she'd fallen asleep in the night before. Self-consciously, Harriet climbed into the tub and shivered as her skin touched the cold surface. She sat down uneasily and tried to remain as modest as she could.

Without ceremony, Nurse dumped the contents of the pitcher straight over Harriet's head. Spluttering and gasping, Harriet pushed hunks of long, wet brown hair out of her eyes.

Just as she was getting her breath back, another stream of water cascaded down her face. For the third assault, she managed to tilt her head back, which at least kept her hair out of her eyes. Nurse began to scrub at her back and hair, cleaning it for all she was worth. Harriet winced as her hair was pulled, hard. Clearly, conditioner was not a thing in the middle ages.

Nurse spoke quietly as Harriet was bathed, talking about this and that. Harriet tried pinching her arm, to wake herself from what seemed like an incredibly vivid dream. She kept pinching until an angry bruise rose on the skin of her arm. Harriet stared at the purpling skin, proof that this situation was very real. Tears welled up in her eyes and panic clawed at her throat. Fear and confusion reigned over her, in stark contrast to the calm that Nurse exuded. The tears ran helplessly down her cheeks, mingling with the water from the pitcher and hiding her distress from Nurse's keen eyes.

Harriet had remained silent as her mind battled to accept what was happening. As her fear quietened under Nurse's soothing touch and her heavily accented voice lulled her, Harriet's tears stopped and she began to focus on her words. Her brain began to make connections as it calmed, and she tried to pick up clues about where she was, what was happening and what she might expect to happen in the coming hours.

"You're very quiet, my Lady," Nurse said. She sighed when Harriet did not respond.

"I know this situation isn't your first choice," Nurse said in an unsteady tone. "But he's a good man and he'll take care of you." Harriet inclined her head stiffly.

"Fifteen is too young for a bride, in my opinion. But what would I know." Harriet's eyes widened at that. Fifteen! "If you'd just agreed to a long engagement with Paris, he would have waited until your sixteenth birthday, at least. Now…well. The wedding's tomorrow and we do what we must."

Harriet's stomach dropped. Clearly, she hadn't dropped into a boring part of the play. Her mind raced as she tried to recall the events leading up to this moment. What had happened to Juliet? Ah. Well. Yikes.

Harriet tried frantically to piece together everything she could remember about the play, every little detail. Romeo and Juliet met at a party. They loved each other at first sight, even though their families were locked in a bitter blood feud. Romeo had snuck into the Capulet Manor to see Juliet and Friar

Lawrence had married them in secret. Romeo had fought with Tybalt, Juliet's cousin, and had killed him. His punishment had been banishment, and if he returned to Verona he would be killed on sight. Juliet had been commanded to marry Paris, kinsman to Prince Escalus. He was handsome and wealthy, but Juliet felt nothing for him. It was all about Romeo. Juliet faked her death, Romeo took his own and was followed into the abyss by Juliet at the loss of her love.

Harriet blew out a breath. What to do? Which part of the story were they currently in. And more importantly, why was she in it? How was she in it? Questions swirled relentlessly through Harriet's brain. She picked up the towel from the edge of the tub and stood shyly, stepping out of the tub and drying herself off as discreetly as possible. She wrapped the towel tightly around herself and turned, only to have her vision abruptly cut off as Nurse threw a shift over her head. Instinctively, Harriet stuck out her arms and managed to find the right holes in the garment. The towel followed the fine material as it slithered down her body, ending below her knees. She whisked her towel off the floor and, with little other option, headed over to the fire where Nurse had seated herself on a chair with a step stool in front. Harriet sat on the stool and Nurse reached out to spread her hair back from her shoulders. She began brushing.

Despite her racing mind, Harriet found herself lulled by the rhythm of Nurse's brush strokes. She was abruptly brought back to earth and her tumbling thoughts when every now and then there was a tug on her long hair.

"Your hair is very shiny and smooth today, Juliet," Nurse said. "There's something different about you today, child. I can't quite put my finger on what it is." Harriet stayed silent as Nurse continued to work on her hair. But after a while, Harriet realised Nurse would almost be finished. She really needed to know more, to try and pre-empt what was coming.

"Nurse," Harriet said in what she hoped was a normal, Juliet-like voice. "Can you tell me what will happen today?"

"Ah, it's hardly surprising that you're nervous, my Lady" Nurse said with a soft smile. *Maybe that is part of the problem,* she thought to herself. "Well. First you will greet some of your guests. They will be here on the nonce." Harriet had no idea what a nonce was, but she went with it.

"Then this evening there will be a ball to celebrate your engagement to Paris. It has been rushed, given the haste of your betrothal, but my Lord says an engagement ball we must have. You will retire early, of course, as tomorrow will be a big day and you need to look your best. As God is my witness, we will not let that beautiful wedding dress go to waste."

Harriet absorbed that information in silence. Married in the morning? She sincerely hoped she was back in Wineglass Bay by then, with her own family and going about her life. But she had no idea how she ended up in what appeared to be 14th century Verona, and even less idea about how to get back home. She had to figure it out. As dire as the situation seemed, the joke was not lost on Harriet. It seemed incredible that she was destined to play out the story of a young woman she considered to be spineless and weak – someone so totally unlike herself that she had no idea how she was going to try to understand her. But she needed to, in order to convince people that she was her. At least until she figured out the best course of action to take.

Although her mind was awash with confusion and nothing quite seemed to align properly, somewhere, deep down, Harriet knew the drawing was the key and she must keep it safe at all costs.

Chapter Three

Harriet sucked in a tight breath. Or she tried to anyway, but the tight corset she had been bundled into made that more than slightly difficult. The day had flown by and it was now evening, time for Juliet's engagement ball. She was no closer to figuring out how to get back to her own time, but she did know that she absolutely loathed Lord Montague.

Juliet's father was a bully. A tyrant who was overbearing and overly used to getting his own way. He had paid Juliet a visit early in the afternoon, after she had greeted a stream of guests staying at the manor, and it was just as well he hadn't realised something was not quite right with his only daughter.

Not that he WOULD notice, he's more about what's good for Lord Capulet, Harriet thought in disgust. No wonder Juliet had ended her life the way she had. Romeo's knife must have looked inviting when she knew she was coming back to someone like that.

Lord Capulet had left Harriet with no allusions about how she was expected to behave. Capulet had ranted about Juliet's behaviour the day before, and Harriet had desperately tried to recall something, anything, from the play that might help her understand what Juliet might have done. He had threatened Juliet with poverty if she made any fuss whatsoever about marrying Paris, underscoring it by gripping Harriet's upper arms viciously to prove his point. That would bruise in the morning, more so than the one she had given herself. He had talked a lot about his reputation, about the Capulet name, and he was adamant that she not do anything to sully that reputation. He spoke about Romeo, telling Harriet that he had been removed as an obstacle and could no longer interfere with the wedding.

The realisation that it was unlikely Capulet knew about the secret wedding between Romeo and Juliet hit Harriet like a bolt of lightning. By her calculations, the wedding had to have happened the night before, or two nights at the very earliest. Harriet now knew roughly which part she had dropped into in the story, which gave her a decent insight into where it was meant to go from here. She tried to decide whether the illicit wedding had happened the same night she had been transported back in time, but her mind raced in circles and she gave up. The last thing she needed was a headache: God only knew how they treated such a minor ailment in the 14th century.

Harriet's attention was transfixed by the throng of people who came into view as she rounded the corner of the sweeping staircase. The butterflies in her stomach went wild, and a few jumped up into her throat. Her hand on the bannister, she baulked at descending into the absolute crush of people at the bottom of the steps. She could see Lady Capulet, Juliet's mother, hovering near Paris' family at one end of the long hall. She'd been introduced to the woman during Capulet's rant earlier in the afternoon and hadn't thought much of her. If ever there was a wife completely under her husband's thumb, it was her.

Lord Capulet was eyeing her coldly from next to the fireplace, scowling and silently communicating his displeasure and control. Juliet must have really pushed her views forward quite strongly to earn such a reaction from her own father. Harriet couldn't understand the relationship that she sensed existed between the two. She knew without a doubt that her own father wouldn't dream of telling her who to marry, let alone speak to her the way Capulet had spoken to his daughter.

As Harriet hesitated at the top of the stairs, she saw a tall, handsome young man with black hair move away from a group of young men at the far end of the hall. He had his eyes fixed on Harriet and was moving towards the bottom of the stairs. Harriet panicked. She assumed this was Paris, given that Romeo would hardly be making a spectacle of himself, according to the play. Harriet noticed that many of the guests had stopped to stare at her, standing at the top of the stairs. Her hair was swept up into a golden net and anchored with the Capulet heirloom band that glittered in the low light from the candles that blazed in the walls and the ceiling candelabras. Her dress, though uncomfortable and strange, was magnificent. The skirts billowed out around her even as she stood still. The gold threads sewn into the rich red material made Harriet appear to glow and the elaborate beading and embroidery on the bodice of the dress gleamed in the light. Harriet had never seen a dress so beautiful. She smoothed her hands down the sides of it, feeling the exquisite material underneath her fingertips.

Harriet steeled herself, drew in as deep a breath as she could in the restricting bodice and started down the stairs. She chanced a look at Lord Capulet and saw his severe expression ease a little, which added weight to her theory that the man heading towards her was Paris. They reached the bottom of the steps at the same time and the man bowed to Harriet, taking her hand in his and raising it to his lips.

"My dear Juliet," he murmured. His liquid brown eyes glowed. Harriet noted the sword hanging at his side and the sash he wore across his dark coat. Even if Harriet couldn't see how handsome he was for herself, the looks that the ladies around them directed his way would have left her in no doubt. "How wonderful it is to see you. I trust you have been well since last we met?"

Harriet mumbled a vague answer as the young man tucked her hand through his arm. They turned and strolled towards the centre of the room, where party guests smiled indulgently at the sight of the pair together. The beautiful, dark haired young lady walking with the dashing and debonair young man, drew quite a bit of attention. The slight age difference between the two didn't appear to bother the guests assembled to celebrate their betrothal. Paris' identity was confirmed in the next moment as a servant hove into view.

"Lord Paris," he intoned. "Lord Capulet requests the presence of yourself and Lady Juliet near the fireplace, if you please."

Paris nodded very correctly at the servant, shrugged lightly and shot a sideways smile at Harriet. He changed course for the fireplace, guiding Harriet along beside him. She was not thrilled with the summons, but knew that it was unlikely she could avoid Juliet's father for long.

Lord Capulet had been joined by his wife and was holding court by the fire. He smiled as Paris and Harriet approached but the expression didn't quite reach his eyes. He inclined his head to Paris and greeted Harriet.

"You look lovely, my dear," Capulet intoned in a humourless voice. Harriet glanced down at the gown she wore. She felt the golden heirloom headband in her dark hair, sitting snug against her scalp to hold the net in place. The red velvet dress shone in the semi darkness, the delicate embroidery and jewels trailing along her arms, winking as she moved. Harriet felt mesmerised if she stared at them long enough. She moved carefully, trying not to trip on the train of her dress that slithered across the stone floor as she moved.

"Thank you, Father," Harriet murmured. That seemed safe enough. She really had no clear idea how people addressed each other in these times.

Capulet moved closer to Harriet and Paris, oozing menace without a great deal of effort. "Paris, Friar Lawrence is ready and willing to perform the ceremony tomorrow," Capulet said, his cold eyes boring straight into Paris' dark brown ones. Harriet felt him shift uncomfortably.

"I know that Juliet is very much looking forward to tomorrow, aren't you Juliet?" Capulet turned his intimidating gaze on Harriet.

"Of course," Harriet murmured, trying to keep a low profile.

"I too," responded Paris, glancing between Harriet and Capulet, registering the strain between the pair that hung in the air, unspoken but clear.

"Juliet, would you care to dance?" Paris asked, as the musicians struck up a new song. Lord Capulet nodded his consent as Paris looked his way. Harriet gratefully accepted and allowed Paris to sweep her away towards the open area reserved for dancing.

Harriet was jubilant to be away from Capulet. She was smugly reviewing how little time she'd had to spend with Juliet's father, until she realised that she was in no way prepared to perform a 14th century partner dance. Harriet looked desperately around, trying to find cues from others around the room. But it looked like they were the first dancers, and everyone else was waiting for them to begin. Harriet's 21st century PE classes had in no way prepared her for this. She knew that she couldn't back out of the dance…Lord Capulet would be all over her in seconds. Faking an illness would get her nowhere, and she wasn't a hugely convincing liar anyway. The only thing for it was to throw herself on Paris' mercy.

"My Lord Paris," Harriet said, hoping that was the proper address. She had heard Nurse addressing Capulet that way earlier in the day. Paris turned his head towards Harriet, raising an eyebrow. "Yes, Lady Juliet?"

"Ah…," Harriet swallowed hard. She couldn't tell him anything. She'd just have to do the best she could. "Never mind."

Paris smiled at her. She mentally steeled herself and took Paris' offered hand as the music began.

It was unlike anything she'd ever done before, and she was flying, completely blind. She remembered that her dance teacher had once said that in partner dancing, the female simply gives the lead to the male and follows his movements. Harriet dearly hoped that was true, and she had no other option anyway so it was worth a shot. She let her body go relatively lax and flowed with the music, her dance training kicking in instinctively. She allowed Paris to move her as he pleased and followed the direction of his feet. The dance was a repetitive one and she picked up the rhythm quite quickly. Before long they were sweeping over the floor, moving as if they danced together regularly. Or at least, Harriet looked like she hadn't just dropped in from five hundred years later.

As the last strains of the music died out, Paris stepped back from Harriet and bowed, kissing her hand.

"Would you care to take a stroll?" Paris asked, as he returned her hand to the crook of his arm. Harriet didn't really have much choice, as he was already steering her clear of the dance floor. Harriet began to register the glances of those around her, and the whispers behind hands as they passed the guests gathered in the ballroom. She really couldn't tell if they were good or bad whispers, and she felt acutely self-conscious. She adjusted the sleeves of the dress that now seemed too tight.

Harriet noticed how Paris greeted people briefly as they were intercepted, but always kept moving, kept walking. Harriet was never in one place for long enough to stumble on her words. She was silently grateful for his thoughtfulness, even though he really had no idea just how much he was helping her.

There wasn't much opportunity to talk as they walked – the ballroom was packed with people and they had to concentrate on avoiding elbows and erstwhile feet on Harriet's dress. Harriet got the impression that Paris had a destination in mind, and she understood when she saw the open doors to what appeared to be a terrace balcony directly ahead. Although they hadn't spoken much, being close to Paris and hearing him speak to those around him soothed the intense nerves Harriet felt about being the centre of attention, and her anxiety about making a fool of herself. She watched in awe as a wineglass appeared in her hand, a goblet really, and she watched the dark liquid inside slush around as she walked. She sniffed at it covertly and laughed a little to herself. Her parents would go ballistic if they knew she was being offered alcohol. Harriet laughed inwardly at the absurdity of that thought. Her parents would be horrified if they knew she'd travelled back in time five hundred years. She didn't think the drinking would really rate a mention in comparison.

Harriet was frankly very surprised that no one had noticed a change in the person they thought was Juliet. The only person who had come close was Nurse, but luckily she had been busy with wedding preparations all day. Neither of Juliet's parents had noticed any change in their daughter, and Harriet supposed that was either very lucky or very sad. Probably both. She couldn't imagine her parents not noticing if someone else did some weird swap thing with her body. That made her wonder if Juliet was indeed in Harriet's body in her time, enjoying the sights of Wineglass. Oh my god. The thought filled Harriet with dread. Was she in Juliet's body, and was Juliet in hers? That was just plain…creepy. There weren't many mirrors in this time, she hadn't seen her own reflection since yesterday. She could look completely different, for all she knew. Perhaps Juliet was somewhere, freaking out just as much as Harriet was, trying to adjust to a time that wasn't hers.

The headache threatened again, so Harriet refocused on her surroundings. Thinking this way wasn't helping much: she needed to figure out how to get home. She had to connect with this story and start thinking of a way out of this.

Paris had steered her onto the balcony, and the air was refreshing after the crowded ballroom. There were a few other couples walking on the balcony, but Paris set out for a secluded corner. He turned Harriet to face him, his face lit with expectation.

"Juliet!" He exclaimed. "It feels like it's been so long since I last saw you." Harriet murmured a reply. The play hadn't had this interaction in it. This was unscripted, and she saw the opportunity to do with it as she saw fit.

She saw Paris was frowning at her. She'd been thinking for too long without speaking.

"Ah…yes, my Lord," Harriet replied. "How long has it been, exactly?"

Paris frowned. "It's Paris, Juliet. I thought we'd gone past that?" He stood, a ponderous expression on his face. "We haven't seen each other in…five days," he said. "I asked for your hand in marriage five days ago, and it was confirmed that afternoon. We saw each other, but briefly. It's never long enough, Juliet."

Harriet was facing the room, her face lit by the candles inside. Since the light was low, Paris didn't see her face register relief as she saw Nurse making a beeline for Harriet through the crowd, and she could only hope that this was the early retiring time Nurse had spoken of. Her hopes were realised as Nurse appeared in front of her, slightly dishevelled.

"Juliet, it is time," she stated, bobbing a curtsey at Paris. "We must go now." Paris' face fell.

"I will see you tomorrow, sweet Juliet," Paris said, disappointment clear in his tone. "Tonight I will stay here, at Capulet Manor, and tomorrow we will be married. We will leave together for my estate after the wedding and we need never be parted again."

Harriet bid Paris farewell and left him on the balcony, following in Nurse's wake, as she swept through the crowded room like a ship under full sail. The crowd parted to let her through and before long, Nurse and Harriet had gained the top of the staircase. Harriet glanced back, searching the crowd for Paris. She saw him – he had come in from the balcony and was watching her walk away. She shot him a small smile and disappeared down the hallway after Nurse. He really was quite a nice guy. Maybe he just wasn't for Juliet.

***

"Well Miss," Nurse burst out as soon as the door to the room was closed. "What have you been keeping from me, then?

And *why?*" Hurt flashed across Nurse's face as her hands settled on her hips. Harriet was caught unprepared and panic gripped her heart. Nurse had worked out that she wasn't Juliet. Harriet felt the reassuring rustle of the paper held securely in the bodice of her dress. She knew instinctively that it was the link to home, she just didn't know yet how to use it. She needed more time.

"Regardless of why you decided not to tell me, everything is prepared and ready," Nurse said stiffly. "It's not my place to question such things." Harriet could see that Nurse was hurt, and she was confused. She would have expected anger, perhaps indignation and certainly a demand to know where Juliet was. She didn't know. They were talking about something else now.

"Ah…" Harriet began. "I didn't want you to be upset, Nurse." She searched Nurse's face for signs of approval or disapproval. Nurse didn't disappoint. Her lips set in an uncompromising line.

"I can't say that I give you my blessing for this Juliet," she said as she advanced on Harriet. Her hands went onto her hips. "But seeing as how you've already married that Romeo Montague, there is little to be done for it. You

must go through with this plan: I really don't
see any way out of it."

Harriet stared at Nurse, her jaw slack. Her
mind raced as parts of the original story
tumbled down around her, and her brain tried
to put them back together, like a giant jigsaw
puzzle.

"Did Friar Lawrence say that Romeo knows
about the plan?" Juliet asked, hoping this was
a reasonable question. From the way Nurse
rolled her eyes, she wasn't too sure.

"Romeo went and got himself banished now,
didn't he! He killed that good for nothing
Tybalt, silly boy. The Friar is getting a message
to him now, the good Lord knows the last
thing we need is the boy doing something
rash." Nurse produced a vial from the folds of
her gown.

"Here is the potion. The Friar says that you
must take this before anyone comes to wake
you in the morning. It will take just minutes to
work, and it will then appear as if you are dead.
The state will last for two days, and on the
third you will wake and Romeo will take you
with him to Mantua. You will not know
anything of what goes on after you take this,
do you understand?" Nurse pushed the vial
into Harriet's hands. Harriet nodded, her eyes

on the dark blue liquid inside the tiny glass bottle.

Nurse took Harriet's face in her hands and looked into her eyes, her own narrowing.

"As I said this morning Juliet, something is different about you." She caught her tongue between her teeth, her eyes searching Harriet's face. Harriet wondered whether to simply come clean with Nurse and tell her she wasn't Juliet. How bad could it be? Then Harriet remembered the one other thing that she had read about this time. Specifically, what happened to those accused of witchcraft. She was pretty sure that for a woman appearing to inhabit another's body, the odds of surviving in the 14th century were not fabulous. She held her counsel.

Nurse moved swiftly, releasing Harriet from the ball gown and throwing a filmy white nightgown over her head. She laced the strings at the front, a little more vehemently than was necessary. Harriet slipped the drawing surreptitiously into her palm and up her sleeve as Nurse dressed her.

"I hope this works Juliet. I hope that you still think it worth it when we're done. Paris really isn't such a bad man, you know," Nurse said. Her face softened and the lines of her many years were more obvious. "But I know your heart is with Romeo, and you must do what needs to be done. Sweet dreams, my dear girl. I hope that this marriage is everything you want it to be."

Nurse looked at Harriet and kissed her cheek. She squeezed Harriet's hand one last time and it seemed as though that might be it; but Nurse began to cry. At first it was little droplets of tears staining her cheeks, and before long her head was buried on Harriet's shoulder, her sobs coming out in great wails. Harriet patted her on the back awkwardly as Nurse's grief poured out of her.

"I've raised you since you were a baby. The good Lord knows what I'll do now. I won't live in this household with Lord Capulet, not without you in it." Harriet didn't know what to say. The enormity of what she was doing crashed around her, clamouring to get inside her and set her emotions ablaze. This was a girl's life she was playing with, as well as Paris and Romeo's lives. And Nurse too, she could now see. Harriet reflected wryly that she didn't think Juliet's mother would have such a violent reaction to her leaving, and she relaxed enough to shift the wailing woman in her arms to make her more comfortable. She murmured soothing sounds as Nurse cried it out, staining the shoulder of Harriet's gown with her tears. Juliet must be quite the person to inspire this kind of loyalty and love.

Eventually, Nurse's sobs quietened and she hiccupped a little. She wiped her eyes on her sleeves and drew back from Harriet's arms, gazing at her face. Harriet's eyes were wet from watching Nurse's pain, and it was enough for the old woman not to ask questions. Nurse visibly gathered herself, steeled her shoulders and squeezed Harriet's hand for the last time.

"Goodbye, my dear Juliet," she said in a husky voice as she let go of Harriet's hand.

Then she turned and sailed to the door, went through it and closed it firmly behind her.

Harriet was alone. She wandered over to the window and sat down on the seat tucked into that corner of the room. She rested her head on the mountain of soft pillows. Harriet had never felt so isolated. And she had roughly ten hours to figure out what on earth she was going to do.

Chapter Four

Harriet sat up on the window seat with a gasp. She frantically searched for the drawing as her mind cleared, and bitter disappointment crept in as she realised she was still in Juliet's time. There had been a part of her that had hoped if she went to sleep with the picture on her, she might just appear back in Wineglass Bay. Panic flooded through Harriet, chasing the disappointment away, as she realised that she had even less time to figure out what she was going to do.

Harriet shook her head as she woke fully, remnants of the dream – vision, whatever it was – that she had just had, circling in her mind. It had seemed as though she was in Juliet's head, in her thoughts, and they had swirled around and around. Time had seemed to fracture, and it was almost like she was seeing a version of events that she couldn't quite remember from the play, but that she didn't know existed in the story she was in either. She mulled that over. Perhaps what she had seen in Juliet's mind had happened, and good old Shakespeare had culled it out. Editorial purposes, you know.

There had been flashes of a wedding, small, with just Romeo and Juliet standing before an altar drowned in candles and flowers. A stern looking old man between them, binding their hands in marriage. A horse ride in the dark of night: fear, confusion and an overwhelming sense of haste swirled around in a cocktail of feelings that were just there, without explanation. The inside of a little cabin in the woods, with a fireplace and a small bed. The happy and content face of Romeo, a man who was clearly in love with his new wife. And Juliet's feelings when she looked at him, as bright as the sun and almost painful to endure. Fear for the man she had married, but overwhelming relief at being together and alive. And so much love.

Harriet had always considered Juliet to be a meek type of woman: someone who didn't fight for what she wanted. But Juliet's actions – the ones she'd just had a glimpse of – weren't those of a timid woman. She had decided to leave Capulet Manor and follow Romeo – how long ago she wasn't sure – consequences be damned. They were the actions of the brave, and possibly desperate:

two people reaching for what they wanted above all else.

But where were they now? The cabin she had seen a glimpse of? And what was she going to DO? That was the most important question at this moment. She could take the potion, but was pretty sure that she knew how that storyline would end. She wasn't confident enough from just a dream that Juliet was with Romeo, or that he had been sufficiently warned that she was faking her death. Did she have the power to change the story? She certainly had the motivation – she was inexplicably tied to Juliet's body, or at least her identity, and she assumed that if it ceased to be alive, so would she.

Harriet was aware of how the original story ended – but would her own, altered version, end any better? And what could she do, here and now, to change it?

Harriet drew her knees up as she sank back into the window seat pillows again, resting her head on them as she mulled over her options. She could run away to Mantua tonight and go to Romeo. Unfortunately, Harriet had no idea how to get to Mantua. Not a viable choice. Neither could she run away anywhere else. She was certain from her interactions with the intimidating Capulet that she would be found swiftly and be brought back to Verona. She expected she wouldn't be dealt with nicely, either. He wanted this marriage between Juliet and Paris, and she sensed that he would do anything to make it happen.

Harriet could summon Friar Lawrence and hope he'd be more open to the notion of time travel than she believed Nurse would be. But what could he tell her that she didn't already know? Harriet understood more than he did, as an observer of the story from the future. His plan definitely wouldn't work, at least not in the state it was now.

But perhaps…perhaps he could help her think of another way. He knew Verona, and these people, in a way that Harriet did not. Her interaction with Nurse had impressed upon her just how crucial this was – she was playing with the lives of many people. She needed help, from someone who knew the individuals she was dealing with.

As crazy as it sounded, Harriet thought Friar Lawrence might just be her best chance of salvation. The problem was, he was an unknown quantity. Although he had played a fairly significant role in Romeo and Juliet, relatively little was known about him. He was what her teacher had called a flat character – someone who doesn't change as the story plays out around him and of whom the reader learns little. Harriet would be in unchartered territory if she summoned the Friar, but she had a feeling she'd be dead in two days if she didn't.

In the corner of the room near the bed, Harriet spied a tasselled rope hanging from the roof. She thought it might be one of those old fashioned bed pulls, like in Cinderella, and the idea of giving that a go definitely trumped wandering the corridors in her night gown clad state. Harriet crossed to the rope and gave it a gentle pull. Nothing happened. She gave it a more definite tug and heard a slight ringing what sounded like a good distance away. It carried on the night air that was still, now that the party had dispersed.

A light knock sounded at the door, and Harriet crossed to it quickly and pulled it open. On the threshold stood a young maid, dressed in a simple black dress. Only a strip of her blonde hair was visible underneath her serviceable white cap, but her face was very pretty and welcoming.

"How may I help you, Lady Juliet?" the girl asked politely. Harriet ushered her inside the room, glancing down the long corridors before she shut the door softly.

"Ah…", Harriet began, trying to find a way to phrase her request that wouldn't arouse suspicion. "What's your name?" Darn. Not a good start.

The girl looked at Harriet, clearly puzzled. "It's Caterina, my Lady," she replied, tilting her head to the side. "Pardon me for asking my Lady, but are you quite alright?" She was studying Harriet as if she had grown another head.

"Yes, quite fine Caterina," Harriet replied, trying to sound normal. "I'd like to speak with Friar Lawrence." She tried for a commanding, confident tone that invited no argument.

"It's awfully late, my Lady," Caterina began. Harriet turned to look at Caterina, and it must have been something in her eyes that made Caterina stammer. "But – but I'm sure that if he knows you'd like to see him, my Lady, he'd make the time." Caterina hurried to the door. "Shall I send him here, my Lady?" Caterina slid the bolt from the door and cracked it open. She looked Harriet up and down, taking in her night gown and bare feet.

"Yes please Caterina, that will do," Harriet said in a slightly imperious tone.

As Caterina scurried away, Harriet reflected on their interaction. She really could get quite used to calling shots and having people actually follow her orders. It certainly wasn't like at home. Harriet fondly remembered all the times her brothers had infuriated her by ignoring even the most politely spoken of her requests. Like the time she was dying for a drink of water and her brother was walking right past the sink, but refused to bring her a glass. Or the time that she was stuck washing and drying all the dishes alone, because her brothers had convinced her parents that it was Harriet who had left dirty plates and cutlery on the coffee table in the TV room.

Harriet slid out of her memories of home as nerves set in again. She began pacing, trying to piece together in her mind how this audience with the Friar would go. She needed a plan, and to make that plan, she needed information. It was really the only chance that she had, the only card she saw that she might have in her hand to play.

Harriet wrung her hands as she paced, putting the puzzle pieces of old and new story together in her mind. Try as she might, they wouldn't all fit together properly.

It appeared it was time to go off script.

Chapter Five

Harriet stood bolt upright at the furtive tap on Juliet's door.

"Lady Juliet?" came an urgent whisper through the door.

Harriet crossed quickly to the door and slid the bolt out of the way. She opened it silently and let the good Friar in.

"Lady Juliet, what on earth are you doing?" Friar Lawrence whispered urgently. He was a heavy set man in a drab brown robe, tied at the waste with a length of rope. His hair was thinning on top and his face was weary and worn.

"What is going on?" the Friar hissed as his eyes scanned around the room.

Harriet attempted to hedge. "Well, Friar, I just – I was just – I just wanted to know how Romeo is," Harriet finished lamely.

The Friar stared at her, incredulous. "Well…he's as good as he can be, I suppose."

Harriet inwardly grimaced. This wasn't going well. "Does…does he know that I'm taking the potion?" Harriet asked.

The Friar scratched his head. "Well, I've sent the messenger off to Mantua to tell him. It's a two day ride by horseback just to get there. My boy should be close to arriving…does it matter?"

"Well…just say, hypothetically speaking, that Romeo doesn't get the message. What do you think he will do?"

The Friar blew out a breath. "It's impossible to say, my Lady. You are expected to arrive in Mantua to meet with Romeo tomorrow." The Friar paused and pursed his lips. "Knowing how reckless Romeo can be, I suppose it is possible that he may react…negatively, if you do not arrive as expected. But it is impossible to say, my Lady. We must go through with your apparent death. It is the only way to get you out of a marriage to Lord Paris, and the only way to make sure that your father does not go after Romeo as soon as you disappear. We know that he will find you too, and drag you back to Verona. He is quite determined to make this match between you and Lord Paris."

Harriet was hanging on every word the Friar said, as her mind frantically tried to plan. It was like jumping off a cliff and assembling a parachute on the way down. She was scared to make the wrong move, to tip Friar Lawrence off to the fact that he wasn't looking at the real Juliet. There was nothing to be gained by freaking out the Friar at this stage.

"So, this potion is our only option?" Harriet asked, stalling for time.

"It is my belief that it is, yes," the Friar said cautiously, unsure where Harriet was going with this line of questioning.

"So…if I left the manor, but I didn't go straight to Romeo, do you believe he will be safe? My father will follow me, not look for Romeo." Harriet stated.

"No, I disagree, my Lady," the Friar said. "Romeo is not safe if you leave because your father will not stop until he finds out his location. You know how ruthless and determined he is. Do you really think that he will let Romeo live, even if he can prove you are not with him? He will find a way to make sure Romeo does not live, even if he has to do it himself."

Harriet absorbed that harsh reality as truth. This was new information, and valuable. Capulet was not a man to be trifled with, which tallied with Harriet's observations. "What will this potion do to me, exactly?"

Friar Lawrence took a patient breath. He had clearly explained this before. "When you take this potion you will not visibly breathe; you will not have a strong pulse. Not strong enough for a physician to find anyway. You will wake from your sleep 24 hours later and go with Romeo. This is the safest way, Juliet."
A fierce internal debate was raging inside Harriet. Her gut told her that this was a disastrous decision. But what else could she do? How could she get around this?
 "Friar, which direction is Mantua?" Harriet asked. The Friar thought before he spoke.
"It's South and slightly West from Verona," the Friar replied. Harriet took a deep breath. She needed more than this merry go round of meaningless talk.
"Friar, Romeo is not going to get the message in time." Harriet's tone was sure and confident. Friar Lawrence looked at her curiously, and not without a little kindness.
"I know you are distressed, my child," he began gently.
"You don't understand," Harriet interrupted. "This is not the whim of some child, or panic at the situation. I know that he will not arrive in time. I know that he will drink the poison you have given him and when I find him dead, I will kill myself with his dagger."

Friar Lawrence's eyes were bulging out of his head. "And how do you know this, my child?"

"I have seen it," Harriet replied simply.

"As in, like a vision from God?" Friar Lawrence said, his face incredulous and tinged with fear.

"This ending will come to pass." Harriet tried to sound authoritative. She didn't miss the gesture the Friar made, crossing himself and running his crucifix through his hands. Perhaps this had been a mistake. It was too late to take it back now, though.

"Whoever takes that potion will be unable to wake for two days, that is all I can tell you," Friar Lawrence said, his eyes darting towards the door. Harriet could see the sweat beading on his brow in the low light. It was time to end this. Harriet had the inkling of a plan forming in her mind – something had sparked with the Friar's last words.

"Thank you, Friar." Harriet folded her hands in front of her dressing gown and hoped that she looked authoritative and in control. "That will be all."

The Friar inclined his head, and with one last, troubled look at Harriet, headed hastily for the door.

"Just remember Juliet," he said as he eased the door open. "You must take the entire contents of the vial for it to be effective. There is a slightly larger dose than is required for your height and weight, but we don't want to take any chances and the extra potion will not have any great impact." With that parting instruction and a nod of his head, Friar Lawrence melted away into the darkened corridor.

Harriet looked after him incredulously. Not have any impact? That was hard to believe, given the potion was designed to slow a pulse enough to be undetectable! Harriet shook her head as she imagined all the other things the doctors in these times thought were effective. Like bloodletting. She shivered. Ew. Perhaps that was why Juliet hadn't woken when she was meant to, why Romeo had killed himself. Well…still didn't explain that part. Harriet couldn't imagine a love strong enough for such a response, despite the flashes of insight she was getting into Juliet's character.

Harriet padded over to the window seat and sat. The heavy curtains were drawn across the window, and Harriet moved them slightly to let the night air and a sliver of moonlight into the room. The beginnings of a plan were formulating in her mind and she was silent as they grew.

Between the candlelight and the weak moon, Harriet was a wraith dressed entirely in white, sitting on the window seat with her legs tucked up underneath her. As the plan grew and her panic subsided, thoughts of home began to creep in. Her head resting on her hand, Harriet stared out through the crack in the curtains at the small sliver of night sky she could see. The stars were so bright without any city lights getting in the way. It was a different sky to the clear, crisp view of the Milky Way she had at home, but it was still beautiful. Sighing, Harriet thought of her parents, and the way that she had left them. She wondered if they were going about their day, if they had noticed that she was gone. Harriet did have a reputation for sleeping in on weekends. It could be hours before they noticed her absence. And her brothers. Lord they were a pain, but she missed them dearly. Here there was no one to talk to, no one to soothe the dread and terror she was feeling. Her friends were no longer just a text away. In fact, she didn't know who her friends were here. The mobile phone that was usually an extension of her arm was nowhere to be seen, and if she wasn't so focussed on surviving, she'd be having withdrawal symptoms. Technology would certainly make contacting the right people much easier just now.

As she watched the stars twinkle against their black backdrop, a reasonable plan began to formulate in Harriet's mind. It was risky, it was dangerous and it could fail horribly. She was scared. She had come to see, from her interactions with the people who knew Juliet, that she was loved. She wasn't so different from Harriet herself – she was just a girl living in a very different time.

As Harriet saw it, her options were presently limited. She had to try something, and it must be done now. She had to be careful. She didn't want to make this worse for Juliet, but doing nothing would achieve no change in the story that was hers.

Turning, Harriet stared at the vial of potion sitting on the bed. Her mind slowly went back over her plan. It should be enough to work. It had to be enough to work.

***

Harriet shivered as her bare feet moved lightly across the dank stone floors of the upstairs corridors. She held a candle to light her way, but it was still as black as the heart of darkness in these hallways. She had traversed the long hallway twice, looking for any signs that might tell her which room belonged to Paris for the night. Two doors still showed a crack of faint light shining from underneath, and she had pressed her ear to the panels of both. She had heard voices in the one furthest from Juliet's room and nothing but silence from the closer of the two. Taking a deep breath, Harriet crossed her fingers and took a deep breath. She had a story ready in case she chose the wrong room, but she hoped it wouldn't come to that.

Paris was startled from his reverie at the light tap on his chamber door. He had been thinking about Juliet, and about their nuptials tomorrow at noon. Puzzled, he looked around for his dressing gown. It was late…and he hadn't called for any of his servants. Paris had met Juliet when she was 13, two years earlier. Although at 16 he was a year older, he had known that she was the one. Lately, she had been a little cold towards him, but after their engagement ball tonight he'd never been as sure of her. She had been like a vision. Although she had been shy and quiet she had dazzled him, leaving him in awe of the girl who was to be his bride. He hoped that, in time, she might come to feel the same way about him. He thought he had seen a spark of that tonight in Juliet's eyes as she looked at him. He had heard a spark of rumours about a liaison between Romeo Montague and Juliet, but the Montague wasn't here and he was.

Paris crossed to the door as the light tap came again. Who on earth could be visiting him at this late hour? It had to be after midnight, and the Capulet Manor lay silent and still. Cracking the door open slightly, Paris' eyebrows shot up when he saw the flash of a white gown and the glow of sable hair in the darkened hallway. The only light came from the torches in the wall brackets lining the stone walls, but they were few and far between. And from the candle held by an insanely nervous Harriet.

"Lady Juliet?" Paris asked, confused. He didn't know what to do. She shouldn't be alone in his room; they were not yet wed. But he couldn't leave her standing out in the corridor. Glancing down, he saw that her feet were bare. His eyes shot back up to her face and he could see her lips were blue. She was clenching her jaw in determination, trying not to let her teeth chatter.

"Lord Paris, may I come in please?" Harriet asked. She hadn't given a second thought to the social customs around being in someone else's bedroom in the dead of the night. Such things weren't at the forefront of her mind in 21st century Australia.

"Ah...," Paris hedged. "Are you sure, Juliet? Shall I come out to you?"

"No, no, there's no need," Harriet said, nudging against the door with her foot. Paris gave way to the pressure and allowed the door to open wider. He watched as Harriet sailed in, her gown sweeping along the floor. She looked confident, but her hands were shaking and her lips trembling. And she was in her night-dress! Paris didn't know where to look. He averted his eyes from her nightgown clad state, as he had been taught a gentleman should. She stopped and turned to him. Paris leant his back against the door to the room, ready to pull it open in a moment should he need to. He was nervous, but hopeful that her appearance in his room meant that her feelings towards him were growing.

"Lord Paris, I wish to speak with you about our nuptials tomorrow," Harriet started, her speech formal, but her tone uncertain. She turned and faced him, her back to the window. Paris inclined his head, inviting her to speak. He was keeping his distance on the other side of the room, unsure about how to handle the situation.

"Perhaps we might have an ale?" Harriet asking, stalling for time.

"Of course, of course," Paris murmured, his manners instinctively driving him to the table at the side of his room. He picked up a pitcher and turned over a cup, then shrugged and turned over another. "I only have small ale; you know how risky the water is. Just the other day my steward was saying it's the worst he's ever seen. With all the plagues going around, you know…," Paris trailed off, realising that he was babbling. He handed the cup to Harriet silently and went back to the table to pick up his own. He downed it in one gulp and poured himself another. He was clearly nervous, and steeling himself for a conversation he hadn't seen coming. Harriet took a small sip of her drink. She tried not to gag as the bitter taste of ale settled on her tongue and assailed her nostrils. She took another, healthier, gulp of the ale and set it down on the small round table near where she was standing.

"Paris," she began, interlacing her fingers in front of her intricate dressing gown. She edged forwards as she spoke, aware that Paris' attention was riveted on her. He couldn't take his eyes off her, despite what he'd been taught about politeness and chivalry.

"I am anxious about the ceremony tomorrow," Harriet said, deciding that at least partial honesty was perhaps the best policy. "Will there be many guests? There seemed to be hundreds tonight."

"Ah yes," Paris said, frowning, slightly puzzled. "There will be hundreds. Between the Capulet connections and my own relatives and retainers, we number quite a few.

But there's no need to be nervous, Juliet," Paris said earnestly, peering into Harriet's face. "It will be just like every other wedding you've ever seen, I suppose. Were you not the attendant for Lady Benicoeur last Spring? I remember seeing you at the ceremony." Paris certainly had recalled seeing Juliet. That was the clinching moment for him, when he had decided it was time to approach Escalus and Capulet about the prospect of a betrothal between himself and Juliet. Although it had ended up rushed, and Paris had no real clue as to why, he wasn't complaining when the end result matched his own goal.

Harriet had been considering Paris' words, a slight frown in her eyes. "Ah...yes. Yes, I was," Harriet replied, continuing to piece together Juliet's character as she played her. "But this time it is us that all eyes will be upon, and with that comes a certain...anxiety," she said. "Do you not feel that also?" she appealed to him.

"Well I suppose I do," Paris said, frowning. "But I know in my heart that I am doing the right thing." He took a deep breath. "This was a conversation I'd planned for tomorrow night, but now is as good a time as any. Juliet, since the day that I first saw you I knew that you would be my wife. I know that we haven't had many opportunities to speak with each other, and that our betrothal has been…hasty. But that doesn't change my feelings. I know my own mind. That helps me to be sure that our wedding tomorrow will be wonderful, even if I too do not relish the idea of standing in front of that many people." Paris pushed back a lock of his dark hair that had fallen into his eyes. He moved fluidly to stand by his own window seat. He didn't sit, as Harriet was still standing. Although he had broken the rules allowing Harriet to be in his room at night, there were others that he followed without even thinking about it.

Harriet was frowning. "See…I don't understand. How can you have possibly known that J – that I was the right person for you when you hadn't even spoken to me? I could have had a shrill voice, or giggled incessantly."

Paris shrugged elegantly. "I just did. And tonight has shown me that I was right. You seem so assured…so mature." He moved a little closer to Harriet, trepidation still showing on his face. Harriet watched him move, knowing that she had to get around to the other side of him to make her plan work. She picked up her cup and pretended to drain the contents, before striding swiftly to where the pitcher and Paris' cup sat. It was now or never: she couldn't stand around and talk all night. Aside from anything else, she knew that there was a chance Paris would eventually figure out that she wasn't Juliet.

Paris watched as Harriet refilled her cup. She turned and made direct eye contact with him, and Paris nervously averted his eyes. He moved to fiddle slightly with a nearby drape. He needed something to do with his hands.

Harriet reached for the cup Paris had used and set down, and she poured ale slowly from the pitcher. As she did, her hand slid out from the long folds of her sleeve and her fingers worked frantically to unclasp the stopper to the bottle of sleeping potion. The cork finally eased free and she splashed the potion in his cup, trying to make her movements look natural. She shoved the empty vial back up her sleeve, hoping that it wouldn't fall out as she returned the pitcher to its place.

"Well," she said brightly. "Tomorrow will be a lovely day, I'm sure." Paris looked up, slightly confused. He was having trouble following the thread of their conversation. "Perhaps we could have a toast to our…union," Harriet improvised. She moved swiftly to Paris and handed him the drugged cup, carefully checking she had the right one. This plan had gone too far for her to still end up the one drugged.

Paris tapped his cup to Harriet's as she held hers out, inviting him to toast.

"To true love," she said, a bright smile on her face. Paris clinked cups uncertainly and raised his own to his lips. Harriet held her breath as he seemed to hesitate, then let it out in a whoosh as he downed the cup in one go.

Paris grimaced as the odd taste slid down his throat. "That's…different," he said, staring at the cup. Harriet watched as realisation dawned on his face, dread in her stomach. This felt awful.

"You…you didn't," he stammered, and he dropped the cup as he stumbled towards her. As he let out a strangled cry, Harriet dropped her own cup and took his arm, guiding him to the side of the bed. She didn't want him to fall and be hurt – he was actually a really nice person, if a little old fashioned in the way he approached love and women. And she certainly didn't want anyone to hear his cries. Harriet glanced nervously at the door.

Paris stumbled backwards, steered by Harriet; his legs meeting the edge of the bed. He collapsed onto the cover. Impulsively, Harriet bent down and grabbed his ankles, swinging his legs up onto the bed as his momentum carried him backwards. Paris' eyes were rolling back in his head.

"Why?" he murmured as the darkness closed in around him.

"I'm sorry," Harriet whispered. "It had to be this way. You will sleep now, but you will wake up. I promise you, Paris." This way was pretty terrible, but at least Paris would wake up in a day or so. His bride would be gone, but at least she wouldn't be dead. And neither would he.

Harriet took a step back from the bed, looking down at Paris' still form. He looked serene in sleep, and a lot younger than she had thought. His handsome face was relaxed and calm, with no sign of the toll that years of living in Renaissance Italy had taken. The harsh conditions and expectations for boys to be men at a young age had made Paris seem years older than he really was. She couldn't imagine the realities of daily life in this time; all she knew was what she'd read in history books. And from what she'd read in her favoured crime thriller novels, she really needed to make this look like Paris had taken the potion on his own and hightail it out of his room.

Swiftly, Harriet positioned Paris' head so he was comfortable. She shook the empty vial out of the sleeve of her gown – a remarkably handy hiding place, as it turned out – and placed it on the floor beside where Paris lay on the bed. She picked it up again to hastily wipe off any traces of her fingerprints, before realising that DNA technology didn't yet exist. She was safe on that front. He had already been dressed in a nightgown, so she didn't have to remove his shoes or anything like that. Thankfully.

Taking a step back, Harriet surveyed the scene. She tilted her head to the side. Something wasn't quite right. Reaching out, she lifted Paris' arm and draped it over the side of the bed. There. Now it looked like he'd dropped the vial after he'd taken it. Perfect.

Hurriedly, Harriet retrieved her cup from where she had dropped it on the floor and tucked it back near the pitcher, along with the cup Paris had used. Straightening the pitcher, she made it look as though the cups hadn't been touched. Then her brain kicked in and she realised that half the pitcher must be missing, so she turned her cup over again and poured a little ale into the bottom of it. Perfect.

Harriet's lungs seized as she heard the sound of voices in the courtyard below Paris' room. They were men's voices, but she couldn't hear what they were saying. They reminded Harriet that she had to get out before she was seen anywhere near Paris' room. Taking one last look at the scene, and directing one last apologetic glance towards the still figure in the bed, Harriet slipped from the room and hurried back to her own.

It was time for the next stage of her plan.

Chapter Six

The sound of thundering footsteps jerked Harriet from the light sleep she'd dozed into on the window seat. She couldn't bear to lie down in the bed and sleep, not after what she'd just done to Paris. She sincerely hoped that the potion acted as it was expected to. She didn't want to hurt Paris, she just needed time to get away from Verona so she could try and fix this unholy mess Juliet found herself in.

A sharp rap sounded at Juliet's door. Her wits re-engaging, Harriet ran and leaped onto the bed, pulling the covers over herself just as Nurse swung the door wide. Harriet sat up, trying to look as sleepy as possible.

"Juliet!" Nurse's eyes widened as she took in Juliet's conscious state. She hurriedly slammed the door shut. "What has happened? We have received word that Paris is dead! And you are…not dead? Oh! Oh, Juliet, what have you done?" Nurse hissed the last words as it dawned on her how Paris was likely to have met his untimely end. "He isn't dead, is he?" Nurse asked, her arms crossed over her ample chest.

"Ah…no," Harriet said, swinging her legs from the bed. "I spoke with Friar Lawrence late last night. He said that there's a chance Romeo hasn't received the message that I am asleep, not dead. Imagine what he will do when he hears the news, or when I don't show up in Mantua today? We couldn't take that risk!"

Nurse stared at Harriet. "So what have you done now, child?" she asked, her face set in rigid lines. Harriet couldn't tell how she felt about the unexpected change in plan. Harriet had spent the wee hours of the morning trying to decide how she would deal with this moment. She knew that it was still too big a risk to tell Nurse the truth. That particular bombshell was reserved for if and when she had no other alternative. A Doomsday option. Harriet winced, and her words came out in a rush. "Last night I went to Paris' room and drugged his ale. He doesn't know why, but he knows that it happened. When he wakes he may be looking for answers, I don't know what he will remember. We must fix this before he wakes, which by Friar Lawrence's calculations will be some time tomorrow. We have a day to fix this, Nurse."

Nurse had been absorbing Harriet's words, a darkening frown on her face. "Well that's the least of our worries just now, dear," Nurse said in an urgent, low voice. "We have a chapel full of people waiting for a wedding, a groom who appears to be dead and a bride in love with another man. How long do you think it might be before your father considers it might have been you who poisoned Paris, to get your own way? Or worse...that Romeo had someone do it. Romeo is still in danger – your father's temper is unmistakable. If he thinks that this was in any way an attempt to stop the wedding on your behalf, well...I wouldn't like to be Romeo in that event. Or yourself, for that matter. Lord, Juliet, you need to show that you're distraught about the death of your betrothed. It's the only way to protect yourself and Romeo from your father."

Harriet's mind swirled. Nurse was right, darn it. Capulet really was an impossible man to deal with, and she wasn't the only one afraid of him. Harriet hadn't missed the uneasy glances between the Capulet staff when it came to Lord Capulet's demands, or the look of horror on a young maid's face the night before when she had dropped a tray in front of him. What should she do? The only people who knew she had the potion were Nurse and Friar Lawrence. She knew that Nurse wouldn't betray her, and she was pretty confident the Friar wouldn't be giving evidence any time soon that he had married Romeo and Juliet in secret. Capulet would have his head for that.

"Juliet, you have to get dressed and go outside – now. You need to be seen, you need to be in mourning," Nurse spoke as she whipped black garments out of the dresser in the corner. She pulled out a black netted headdress from the back of the cupboard and said, "Yes, this shall do nicely. Come now Juliet!"

Harriet hurried over to where Nurse was assembling her outfit. She squeaked in surprise as Nurse whisked the nightgown off and threw the voluminous black dress over her head. Harriet couldn't see a thing as she struggled to find the right way to wear the heavy dress. She could feel Nurse tugging at the hem of the dress and with a swish, the heavy gown fell down to the floor around Harriet. Nurse, still quite nimble for an old, heavyset lady, nipped around behind Harriet and began to tie her laces. Harriet grunted spontaneously as Nurse expertly tightened the ribbons, reducing Harriet's freedom to breathe. As she worked, she spoke.

"Paris' family are looking for answers, Juliet. You must be very careful what you say, and to whom. His family have been informed – Lord Paris' man found Prince Escalus and his men on the road, on the way to the wedding. Given how powerful the Prince is, this could get very complicated, very quickly. It is hard to believe a young man such as Paris would kill himself the night before the wedding he wanted so badly, and his family will think so too. I implore you, Juliet. Be careful."

Harriet stood in front of Nurse, swathed from head to toe in black. The trepidation on her face was shielded as Nurse settled the long black veil in front of Harriet's face. Her features were screened from anyone who cared to look.

"You will still need to do your best to look upset, Juliet," Nurse reminded her. "You can still be heard, and you can see the outline of your face through the gauze."

Harriet nodded to show she had heard Nurse. She slid her feet into the shoes settled near the rug on the side of the room. They were a little tight and pinched her toes, but they were better than running around on cold stones barefoot.

"You are ready," Nurse announced. She gripped Harriet's forearms through the heavy lace sleeves. "You may tell your father that you have been informed of Paris' death so that I may dress you appropriately, but beyond that you know nothing. You don't know where he is, or when it happened. Remember that Juliet – it is important for us all." She released Harriet, turning her towards the door and giving her a little nudge.

Harriet walked forwards, drawing her chin up and setting her back a little straighter. She had set this plan in motion and now it was moving forward, irrevocably and unscripted. She had taken Shakespeare's tale and twisted it, and they were now in unchartered territory. She had a part to play. She had a father to convince. People's lives depended on it.

***

Lord Capulet halted abruptly before Harriet's still form. He had been prowling the floor of the library, where he had taken Harriet as soon as she appeared at the bottom of the main staircase. Capulet had informed Harriet, unfeelingly, that Paris appeared to be dead. Harriet remained silent, relying on her veil to screen her face.

"Do you have anything to say?" Capulet demanded.

"It is awful," Harriet murmured. Her mind was whirling, and Capulet was the epitome of intimidation. He had a look of tightly controlled anger on his face and he regarded her suspiciously.

"You haven't asked how he died, Juliet," Capulet said softly. "Perhaps you already know." He circled around behind Harriet menacingly. She remained silent.

"Juliet. I know you didn't want this marriage. Tell me, right now, is this Montague's work? Did you have anything to do with the death of Paris?" Capulet's face brooked no arguments.

"Father, how could he have?" Harriet asked, trying to appeal to Capulet through the many folds of material in front of her face. "Romeo is not here, in Verona. He's been sent from the city. How could he have arranged this? And why would either of us want to make you angrier?" Harriet was glad that Capulet couldn't see her face. She was sure there was guilt written there, as plain as day. She focussed on trying to keep it out of her voice. Capulet looked satisfied for a moment.

"Yes, the banishment was quite effective," he said. Capulet began pacing again, his boots ringing on the stone floors and echoing up the impressive walls of books. He was an imposing man and he towered over Harriet.

His black doublet and tunic with its fur trimming showed his respects for the passing of a guest under his roof. It also made him appear darker, more threatening, than he did in his usual dress.

"I hear talk that you received a visitor late last night, Juliet," Capulet said, altering his course to circle around Harriet again. Harriet's mind blanked. She hadn't expected this. How could he know so swiftly?

"Ah, yes Father," replied Harriet, stalling for time.

"Friar Lawrence was called to your chamber just before midnight," Capulet continued, watching Harriet carefully. "He left shortly after. Can you explain to me why that was?" Capulet's tone had turned dangerously quiet, but his face showed the menace that lurked underneath. He was encouraging Harriet to speak, yet she knew if she did all hell would break loose. She had to dissemble effectively. She had to put Capulet off wanting to continue this conversation.

"Well Father," Harriet began. Her mind whirled as she plotted her intricate course through these fraught waters, relying on her knowledge of all the things she knew her own father would be uncomfortable discussing. "The Friar is well known for his knowledge on matters of childbirth. Seeing as how I was to be married today, I wanted to make sure…," Harriet's voice trailed off as Capulet flung a hand in the air, imperiously gesturing for her to stop talking.

"Enough. I won't hear any more of this. It is an improper conversation between a father and daughter!" Harriet breathed a sigh of relief.

"Well, you did ask me Father," Harriet said, wicked humour twinkling in the eyes that Capulet could not see behind the veil.

Capulet frowned. "There is speculation that Paris ended his own life, perhaps due to the lack of regard you display towards him. Others say that he changed his mind and could not go through with the wedding. One of the lady servants in his household has been particularly vocal this morning on that front. It is quite insulting. I have an audience with Prince Escalus as soon as he arrives, he will know that I will not hear any more of this blasphemous talk from his household!" Capulet's voice had gotten louder as he spoke, and the colour in his face was high. Harriet was relieved that his attention appeared to be shifting.

"Paris' cousin will answer to slander upon my household and kin," Capulet declared, turning away from Harriet to rest his hand on the marble mantle above the fireplace.

Harriet breathed a sigh of relief and decided to say nothing, preferring instead to fade into the background as much as possible. She watched as Capulet continued his tirade, continued to curse Paris and his kin, even as Lady Capulet strode into the room and slammed the door closed, angrily informing her husband that half the house could hear him ranting.

As Lady Capulet stood beside her husband, she nodded approvingly at Harriet's dress. "Very fitting, my dear," she said, adjusting her own black headdress. Unlike Harriet's, Lady Capulet's veil did not cover her face entirely. Harriet could still see Lady Capulet's features and expressions, and just now she was less than impressed with her husband. But in Harriet's estimation, entirely unlikely to do anything effective about it.

"My Lord," Lady Capulet beseeched Lord Capulet. "Every guest between here and the road to Mantua can hear you. Calm yourself! A young man is dead, Juliet's groom is gone!" Capulet rebuffed her in a quieter, but staggeringly vicious tone.

"Have some pride, woman!" He declared. "Escalus and his kinsmen put a scourge on our household when they allow their servants to talk of Paris changing his mind about marrying Juliet. I will not stand for it! No kin of mine would use such a dirty, dishonourable way of killing a man. Montague, on the other hand…", Capulet paused, his train of thought interrupted. But another thought occurred to him just as rapidly.

"With one groom dead in the ground, how we will convince another to marry her! This talk must stop at once. When this has all blown over, we can look again for potential suitors for Juliet's hand. She wasn't really on offer the first time, Paris got in before the more eligible gentlemen really started to notice her."

Harriet stared at Capulet, absolutely and totally offended. Even though she wasn't Juliet, she was outraged and insulted on her behalf. Really! Is this how 14th century women were treated? Well, she supposed it was. Oh, the history books mentioned that women didn't really have a voice and were the property of the men in their families. But reading about it five hundred years later and seeing it in real time were two very different things. Harriet felt an affinity with Juliet, wherever she currently was. She couldn't imagine her father speaking about her as if she were a prized cow for sale. And she definitely could not see her mother being alright with him doing so! But Lady Capulet did not disagree with her husband, nor did she admonish him for the way he referred to his daughter. She simply stood there, a pensive look on her face and a frown in her eyes. Harriet decided to end her silence.

"You know Father," Harriet began. "There is one other gentleman who would marry me." As soon as the words left her mouth, Lord Capulet was swinging around.

"You will not dare to speak the name of that boy in my house again," he spat as he rounded on Harriet. "It is bad enough that an entirely suitable, wealthy and powerful gentleman has been found dead on the day of your marriage to him. To marry you to Montague would ruin us entirely." Capulet's booming voice was back, and Lady Capulet hurried to quieten him.

Harriet decided it was too good an opportunity to pass up. "Why is there such bad blood between our families?"

Capulet turned an alarming shade of purple. Lady Capulet shook her head at Harriet and pursed her lips.

"Why…why? You ask me why that vile family are our enemies?" Capulet thundered, shaking off his wife's desperate pleas for him to be silent. "Lord Montague has been the bane of my existence since I was a lad. He's a good for nothing wastrel. He's…he's…" Capulet was running out of words. Harriet didn't know if that was because of his rage or because he truly could not actually articulate why he hated the senior Montague so badly.

"I just do, Juliet. And you had better begin accepting that there will never be a future for you with that good-for-nothing son of his. No daughter of mine will become a Montague. I would kill you both first." Capulet swung away from Harriet. "I can assure you, girl, you will be locked in that room of yours if you put another toe out of line, and you can stay there forever." Capulet settled near the fireplace, staring moodily into the flames. His shoulders rose and fell with angry breaths and his fists were clenched at his sides. Lady Capulet glided towards her husband, catching Harriet's eye as she moved. She motioned her head towards the door, encouraging her to leave the room.

Harriet didn't need to be told twice. She walked as calmly as she could to the door, opened it quietly and slipped out into the corridor. Closing the door, she rested her back against the stone wall next to it for a moment as she caught her breath. She realised that she was shaking, and she could absolutely see why Juliet would be afraid of her father. Harriet could feel the adrenaline flowing through her veins and the tremors in her hands. She pressed her palms against the cold wall, steadying herself.

Her plan was in motion, and the chips were raining down. Harriet was frantically trying to stay a step ahead of the game – ahead of the story that she knew was breathing down her neck. She didn't truly believe in fate…at least in a fate that couldn't be controlled or influenced. Harriet firmly believed that if you wanted something badly enough, and if you worked hard enough for it, there was a very good chance you could get it. She supposed she got that from her own mother.

She knew that Juliet desperately wanted to be with Romeo. She understood more with each passing hour how strong that desperation must be, if Juliet was willing to risk so much to marry him. Harriet mentally shook herself and pushed away from the wall. She had to stay focussed. This tale hadn't ended yet. She still had some influence to use, and a good dose of 21st century empowerment and belief behind it. Plus, a knowledge of how the story was meant to end didn't hurt at all. Pretty much anything she did at this point seemed like it would be an improvement. Harriet took the wide staircase hurriedly, nodding sombrely at those who passed by. She didn't linger long enough to look at their faces. Striding down the corridor, Harriet spied the door to Juliet's room. At least that was one place she would be safe. The passages within the manor certainly were not.

Passages. Roadways. Harriet stopped in her tracks. "…*Every guest between here and the road to Mantua can hear you. Calm yourself! A young man is dead, Juliet's groom is gone!*" Harriet's eyes widened as Lady Capulet's words rang in her head. The road to Mantua. The road to Romeo. And she hoped, the road to freedom. Her approach would need a little refining, and it was definitely a risky option. But in this case, the gamble might pay off. If she stayed, there was no telling what Capulet might do. He could make good on that threat to lock her up and she would be useless to everyone. And how would she get to Paris before the potion wore off? She would have to explain. And to do that, she needed to escape the Capulet Manor. It might make Juliet look guiltier, but that would happen when Paris awoke anyway. She had to get to Mantua and try to find Romeo, before it was too late for them all.

And she knew just the person to help her get to Mantua.

Chapter Seven

Harriet tugged on the bell pull in the corner of her room, before turning and hunting wildly for something, anything – a bag, clothes, money – to travel with. Her dense black skirts swished around her and tangled her legs up if she tried to move over a certain speed. Blowing out a frustrated breath, Harriet untangled her limbs and mentally ordered herself to slow down.

She opened the cupboard she knew Nurse used to store Juliet's clothes. She crowed with delight as she saw a small brown box in the back of the cupboard, sporting what looked like brass buckles and a thick strap. Harriet yanked on the strap, causing an avalanche of shoes, hair combs, scarves and God knows what else to tumble out onto the floor. She winced at the noise, then stepped gingerly over the top of the tangled mess into the centre of the room. Harriet laid the case onto the floor and glanced around the room before remembering there was definitely no clock here. Peering out the window, she estimated it was about 10 o'clock in the morning. Not that Harriet had a great deal of experience in telling the time by the sun, living as she did in a world with iPhones, wristwatches and laptops. But it was the best she could do just now.

A knock sounded at the door. Harriet stepped over to it and pulled it open. Caterina, the maid from the evening before, stood framed in the doorway. She bobbed a curtsey as she saw Harriet, crossed herself and murmured, "I'm sorry for your loss, my Lady. May God save his soul and purge it of sin."

"Yes, yes," Harriet said impatiently, taking Caterina's hand and pulling her into the room, before slamming the door shut. Caterina just stared at where Harriet's hand lay on her arm. Harriet saw and quickly dropped her hand. "Ahh…yes. Thank you Caterina. It was quite a shock to wake up to this morning." Harriet knew that she needed to remember she was acting a part, and Juliet was meant to be distraught at the loss of Paris.

"How can I help you, my Lady?" Caterina asked, her hands folded neatly in front of her white apron.

"Yes, I need to summon Nurse. Do you know where she is?" Harriet asked. Caterina frowned.

"Friar Lawrence called for her a while ago, actually," Caterina said. "I think they left the manor, but when they'll be back I don't know. Can I help?"

Harriet put her hand over her eyes, rapidly trying to re-evaluate the situation.

"You have no clue where they went?" she said, dropping her hand to her side. Caterina could sense her frustration and anxiety.

"No, my Lady. But I'm sure whatever it is, I can help. You know I can," Caterina added earnestly. "Pardon me, my Lady…please don't think me impertinent, but what will you do now that his Lordship has passed away?" She crossed herself again. "I know that your mother has taken care of the guests in residence, who are mostly leaving tomorrow morning. There will be no viewing of the body, given the circumstances of his death, and Paris will be laid to rest later tonight. The kitchens are in a frenzy over turning a wedding into a wake, especially for a potential suicide. It's hard to make some of it look less…festive, though." Caterina halted, unsure of her ground and aware that she had been chattering away like a monkey. She looked up and saw Harriet regarding her steadily.

"I am so sorry, my Lady," she stammered. "I meant no offence." Caterina bustled over to the cupboard, hurriedly scooping up trinkets from the floor where Harriet had tumbled them. She was anxious and clearly trying to keep her hands busy. Harriet wasn't even thinking about Caterina's words. Rather, she was thinking about the way that she had said them. There was clearly a level of regard between Caterina and Juliet – the maid had felt comfortable enough to ask such questions, after all. Perhaps Caterina would be the perfect person to let in on her situation. Unless she had been the person who told Capulet about the Friar's visit. Harriet frowned. She bit her finger as she thought frantically, but decided to take a chance that there was a confidence between the two women and Caterina was innocent of tipping off Capulet.

"Caterina, forgive me. I've had so much on lately we haven't had much time to talk." Harriet crossed her fingers behind the folds of her gown and hoped she was on the right track.

"Oh no, my Lady," Caterina said, relief clear in her voice. "You've had much bigger things to worry about than what I've been doing!" So there was a relationship here. Teenage girls did indeed flock together, no matter which time they hailed from.

"No, I'd like to know," Harriet said, stooping down to pick up a long length of material and beginning to fold it like she had seen Caterina do. She tried to calm her racing heart and the impending sense of a ticking clock that she felt keenly.

"Well…it's just like always!" the little maid burst out. "It's all about what men want! It's about my father's wishes, and my brother's ideas. God forbid I should have some ideas or wishes of my own! No! I'm a woman, so what I want doesn't matter." Caterina shook her head. "There has to be more than this," she finished, placing a pile of clothes neatly back into the cupboard. Harriet considered that. Then she jumped in head first.

"Oh there is," Harriet replied. What did she have to lose? Well, quite a lot, but she also had a great deal to gain. "Do you know the way to Mantua, Caterina?"

"Well, of course," Caterina replied, turning to put another stack of material into the cupboard. "My brother takes me there once a month to trade his stock. At least until he gets the shipping company up and running." Caterina stopped talking and slowly swivelled. Her shrewd eyes took in the mess still littering the floor before sweeping over to take stock of the open leather case laying in the middle of the rug.

"I see," she said softly. "You want to go to Mantua. That's why all of your belongings are on the floor. That's why you're looking for Nurse. Juliet. Juliet, please. Take me with you. There has to be more to life than doing what my father and brother say, and it's only a matter of time before they marry me off to Paolo. I can't think of anything more repugnant. He is a pig of a man," Caterina spat, her eyes sparking. "He's not even bothering to hide the fact that he will destroy my brother's business if I don't marry him. In fact, he's using it as his bargaining chip."

Harriet could see why. Caterina, although dressed in the drab garb of a household servant, was quite clearly a very beautiful young woman. Her hair was like liquid gold under the white cap of service and her skin was smooth, glowing with a light tan. Combined with Caterina's intense blue eyes, Harriet thought that she looked as though she wasn't entirely of native Italian heritage. She shook her head, bringing her attention back to the moment.

"Juliet, please," Caterina pleaded with Harriet. "You know Paolo. He is the last man on earth I would choose to marry." Caterina shuddered. "Please…let me go with you. I don't even care where we're going, or why. If you need to get to Mantua I will take you there. I have access to the stables, I can prepare everything we need. I'll even help you pack! Please, take me with you."

"Well…" Harriet hesitated, not wanting to appear too eager to accept Caterina's help. She was desperate, but she didn't want the little maid to know that. Not only didn't she know the way to Mantua, but she had to get past the staff and her father's men in Capulet Manor. "I suppose you could accompany me to Mantua. But you must not tell anyone and I cannot guarantee what we will find when we get there, or if and when we'll be back." Harriet held her breath. She needed the little maid to accept.

Caterina's eyes glowed. "*Perfect,*" she breathed. "Give me one hour. I will return to fetch you and I will have horses to take us where we need to go. You won't regret this, my Lady, I promise you." With that, Caterina hurried to the door. She turned and gifted Harriet with a beatific smile before she yanked open the door and disappeared from sight. Harriet listened to the latch click back into place. Then she began to furiously stuff clothes into the little case. She had no idea what she needed in this time, but she would make it work. She didn't intend to be here much longer. She would find a way back to her home.

Harriet hurried over the bed and slid her hand under the pillows. Her fingers found the paper of her drawing and she pulled it free of the linen. Smoothing the surface, she looked down at the sketched lines of her own face melded with what she thought was Juliet's.

The original plan had been to make as few waves as possible while she figured out a way home. But things had changed and it wasn't just Harriet's life on the line anymore. She couldn't leave Paris without an explanation, and she'd changed too much of Juliet's story. She didn't want to leave her in danger.

Nevertheless, it was crucial that she keep the drawing safe. There was a part of Harriet's intuition that was screaming it was her ticket back to Wineglass Bay. If she lost it, she too would be lost.

***

Harriet sat on the window seat, her brown leather case tucked out of sight behind the drapes, almost empty despite her frenzy of packing. She had decided to travel light in the end. Harriet certainly didn't want any unexpected visitors to see her prepared for flight. She had searched through Juliet's cupboard for something – anything – that would be easier to travel in than the heavy black dress she currently wore. She had been disgusted to find nothing but fancy dresses and floaty nightgowns. Harriet sighed. The dress would have to stay. She had the drawing tucked into her arm sleeve – really, the best invention ever – to keep it safe and close.

Harriet's nerves came alive as a clock in the square tolled the turn of the hour. It was time, and Caterina should be here any moment. Harriet was attuned to any sound from the corridor, to any noise down in the square. She was acutely aware of her surroundings as she sat restlessly, tapping her fingers on her leg. She looked up sharply as the door to the room burst open without warning. Caterina swung through the opening and nimbly shut the door behind her.

"Juliet," she hissed urgently. "We need to go. The lad I arranged to stay with the horses can only spare a few minutes, and the mass for Paris starts in half an hour. We need to get you out of that gown! You'll be recognisable all the way down the road to Mantua." Caterina reached behind her and pulled out a second gown, much like her own, that she had tucked into her apron. It was drab and brown – it certainly wasn't going to draw extra attention to Harriet, unless they were looking for someone to wash the dishes.

Caterina motioned her over and Harriet strode quickly to her. Caterina spun her around and fell onto the laces, her fingers flying as she deftly unlaced the straps binding Harriet.

In a matter of minutes, Harriet stood in the serviceable brown gown, her drawing tucked up a new sleeve. Caterina hadn't spied the paper, as she had been rapidly returning the room to its previous state. There was nothing here to suggest anyone had left, let alone in a hurry.

"Let's go," Caterina said, scooping up Harriet's travel case from its spot behind the curtains. Harriet had no idea if the contents would be of any use to her – all she was really interested in protecting was the drawing.

Caterina cracked open the door to the room and checked the corridor. Finding it empty, she motioned Harriet through and they ran together towards the spiral staircase at the end of the hallway. Harriet was running blind: she had no idea how to get around the Capulet Manor. She'd seen very little of it as she had been ferried from place to place over the last day. But Caterina was a different story. It was like she had been raised running all over the big house, as she darted into little nooks and crannies and down sideways passages. She stopped and motioned for Harriet to stay still as she ducked through a doorway, nimble and light. She was back within the minute, re-tying the strings on Juliet's travel bag.

"Just something for later," she whispered. "I put it next to your jewels." They had been the only currency that Harriet could think of. As they hurried past the open doorway, Harriet saw it was a chamber off the kitchen that Caterina had slipped into.

Caterina moved with the confidence of someone who knew exactly where she was going, and Harriet supposed she probably did. She had no idea how long Caterina had worked for the Capulets, nor really that much else about her. She knew she had a brother and a father, but that was about it.

Harriet focussed on not tripping on her skirt as they moved swiftly through the dank and darkened stone passageways. She watched the way that Caterina kicked it out of her way as she walked and tried to emulate her movements. Here and there, flaming torches blazed in their wall brackets, lighting the way for a few steps before the gloom fell again. Harriet struggled to adjust her eyes to the low light, lifting her feet high to avoid stumbling on uneven cobblestones. She raced after her fleet footed guide, her breath beginning to come out in uneven pants. Running in a dress, servant style or not, was a lot harder than she had expected.

Ahead, Caterina nipped down a small passageway to the right, disappearing from Harriet's view. It looked as though she had disappeared into thin air. Harriet slowed as she approached the spot where her friend had disappeared, then let out a small squeak as a hand reached out and grabbed her arm, yanking her into what looked like a dingy stone cavern. Caterina pressed a finger to her lips, motioning urgently for Harriet to be silent. Harriet pressed her lips together firmly and listened, trying to determine what Caterina was hiding from. She didn't have long to wait.

Footsteps sounded in the corridor they had just been running through – heavy, ringing footsteps.

"I tell you, Matteo," a deep, unfamiliar voice said. "Capulet has lost his mind. He thinks I am spreading lies about the young Lady. I know not where these rumours come from!" The exasperation in the man's tone was clear.

"Well, my Lord," replied a patient, measured voice. "Capulet is a…difficult man, to be sure. But right now he is upset and his daughter is grieving. We mustn't be too hard on him. I'm sure that after Paris' burial this will get easier."

"This isn't easy on me either, you know!" The frustrated voice was back. "My own kinsman…poison. I simply don't believe it. I miss him," the first voice said sadly. "He was an easy man to be around. I am truly sad that his life was cut so short. He was so looking forward to marrying young Juliet, I know that he has desired it for nigh on two years now."

Caterina looked at Harriet in their hiding place in the tunnel. She winced slightly as she saw the haunted look in Harriet's eyes. She misconstrued its meaning, but she squeezed her arm in solace all the same.

"The young lady will marry again," the second voice said. "And we must honour Paris with all due ceremony and circumstance while we get to the bottom of what happened to him. I do not believe that he took his own life, not Paris. His body is being prepared for viewing at the Church of Sant'Anastasia and he will later be interred in the family vault. We have much to do before the viewing this afternoon. Come, my Lord Escalus. Cast Capulet from your mind, his rantings can do very little to harm you."

The footsteps became fainter as the two men reached the other end of the corridor and disappeared from hearing.

Caterina stuck her head out of the gloomy hole they were standing in. "We are clear," she said, whisking Harriet out into the light. They hurried on as Harriet's mind swirled and guilt churned in her stomach. What would happen if Paris didn't wake in time, before he was interred? Hurting someone else hadn't been part of her plan.

Harriet sucked in her breath and her thoughts stopped abruptly as her eyes were assaulted with a blinding white light. Caterina had yanked open a door and light flooded into the gloomy hallway. Little rainbow dots swam in front of Harriet's eyes, sort of like what happens if you look into a hot afternoon sunset for too long without shifting your focus. Harriet threw her hands out in front of her, trying not to run into anything that might give her a bloody nose. She felt Caterina grasp one of her hands and pull her through the doorway before the door slammed shut at her back.

"Sorry, my Lady," Caterina said, before she whistled, a short, sharp blast of sound. The clatter of clopping hooves on stone followed almost immediately after. Harriet's eyes were slowly adjusting to her new surroundings and she could see they were in a sort of back alley. Lines with billowing white sheets on them almost surrounded where they were standing. There was a narrow space next to the building and from around the corner came a young boy leading two horses single file, the one behind tied to its mate in front.

Nerves swam in Harriet's stomach. She'd only ridden a horse once, and that couldn't really be called riding. Her father had been doing some work at another firefighter's house once during the school holidays and he'd taken Harriet and her brothers along to see the horses. He'd had to, as their mother was never home for the holidays. Harriet had ended up mucking out the horse stalls while her father had worked, before the owner had come to see if they'd like a ride on one of the more docile horses. Her brothers had whooped with delight and jumped straight on, but Harriet had been a little more hesitant. Eventually she'd given it a go when she'd seen her brothers were unharmed. It was a deceptively long way down from the back of a horse.

Harriet's lips quirked as she remembered her father's experience with the horses that day. It had been decidedly less glamorous. Logan Hunter had chosen to ride the little Shetland pony out in the back paddock, in an attempt to show Harriet that horses were safe. The little black pony was called Jellybean, and he had given Logan more than he'd bargained for. As soon as Logan was seated bareback the little horse had taken off. Logan's feet may have been able to touch the ground, but he certainly hadn't enjoyed a smooth or safe ride. He had bailed into a nearby bush as Jellybean ran towards one of the barbed wire fences, but the little pony had veered off at the last minute and sauntering into the safety of his plush green paddock. He had been smugly cropping grass by the time Logan's children reached their father, falling about in stitches of laughter.

If only there'd been iPhones then, Harriet mused to herself. She wouldn't have minded showing her mother that particular little episode. She remembered how she'd left her own time, in a fresh conflict with her mother, and she felt shame and sadness.

Harriet's attention snapped back to focus on a horse much larger than little Jellybean as it halted in front of her. The saddle on its back was beautiful – large, leather and opulently embroidered.

"I couldn't find your saddle, my Lady," Caterina said with a frown. "Nor was Star in her stall. But Raspberry here has a very similar temperament to your own horse and the saddle is your mother's old one. I thought it would do in the circumstances." Harriet nodded her thanks, not trusting herself to speak. Her mouth had dried completely and nerves set gigantic butterflies free in her stomach. She watched as Caterina swung comfortably up into her saddle, sitting sideways on the horse. What on earth was that? Harriet quickly studied how Caterina was perched as the little maid adjusted her skirts, settling them comfortably around her.

"Let's go, Juliet," she said. "We must be away from here – now. We have no idea how long it will be before someone comes looking for you. It's noon as it is, and we have days to ride before we reach Mantua."

Harriet was definitely not looking forward to that part, especially since from hereon out, she was winging it when it came to finding Romeo Montague. But there was no time to start like the present, especially if lingering meant she could get caught. She put her foot in the stirrup and, hoping she was doing it right, swung herself up. She started as the horse shifted beneath her, dancing sideways as her weight settled on its back. Gingerly, Harriet shifted herself around to sit in the side saddle, trying to spread her skirt out so that she wasn't sitting on miles of fabric and her legs didn't feel trapped. She managed to ease her discomfort a little and she caught the reins as Caterina threw them to her.

The maid manoeuvred her horse through the little alley way, and Harriet blindly followed, hoping that the pressure of her feet on the horse's flank was enough to keep her moving. She glanced around her as they went, intensely conscious of how close they were to the walls of Capulet Manor. The throng of people in the square went about their business, hardly glancing their way as the horses picked their way through the crowds. There were too many people packed into one place for any one person to pay much attention to another. Harriet held her breath, hoping there was no hue and cry, at least not before she was free of the restricting crowds.

She breathed a little easier as they joined a line of other horses and carts making their way out of the manor's keep. She could see a fork ahead, with several different roadways branching off in different directions. The Romanesque roads were still intact, still in use by new generations as they had been over a thousand years before. Harriet had studied Ancient Rome when she first started high school and had loved it. She remembered a great deal from that period of time – less so about the impact the Romans had on towns further away from their capital – but she recognised the distinctive stonework nonetheless.

Harriet watched as Caterina swung her horse onto the road, taking the option lying to the left of the fork that looked less worn than the others. The hooves of the animals rang on the cobblestone roads as they walked sedately away from the house of Capulet, not appearing to be in any particular hurry. Harriet's heart stopped as a hail sounded from behind them – a male voice raised towards them.

Caterina turned her horse, shielding Harriet behind her at the same time. Harriet instinctively averted her face from the man who was talking in rapid fire Italian. The cap Caterina had given her helped to hide her hair, but a good look at her face would be their undoing.

Caterina swung her horse back around and continued down the road to Mantua, her hand on Harriet's reins. "He was saying hello,"

Caterina murmured. "We need to move faster once we're out of view."

Harriet was adjusting to the sway of her horse and Raspberry appeared to be a timid mare so far. She was gentle and patient, and she didn't spook easily, which was a major benefit in Harriet's estimation. Caterina's horse seemed a little livelier. The mare shook her head and danced sideways on occasions, requiring Caterina's attention and control to stay seated and on course. Harriet was thankful for calm Raspberry as she watched Caterina wrestle with the mare a little way down the road.

"She's a spirited one," Caterina said, turning to smile at Harriet. "I'm thankful that she's necessary for our family's business or I'd never be able to afford to keep her. She doesn't always like to do what I want to do, but she's learning. And she keeps things interesting, don't you Marmalade?" Caterina stroked the horse's silky chestnut mane and the pretty mare tossed her head and whinnied, seemingly in agreement. Caterina laughed, her eyes alight.

Raspberry and Marmalade. Both horses were named after jams. Was that a coincidence? Where had Caterina gotten this horse from? Did she want to know? Marmalade was clearly Caterina's horse. The two had an affinity with each other that only came from time and experience. Marmalade wore a saddle that was much more worn and plain than the one Harriet sat on, but it was beautifully worked nonetheless. Caterina saw Harriet staring, frowning, at her saddle.

"This was a gift from Paolo," Caterina said, tapping her fingers on the fine leather seat. "It's beautiful, and I'm glad that Alfie accepted it on my behalf or I'd be riding bareback. Although, my brother didn't take it because he thought I'd like it, but to further the alliance between our family and Paolo. Nevertheless, I love it and I'll be sad to lose it." Caterina stopped talking, aware that Harriet hadn't said anything in some time.

"So, how far to Mantua?" Harriet asked, trying to make her question appear light hearted.

"Oh we have a way to go yet," replied Caterina. "It's two days ride from Verona to Mantua, and we're midway through this one. We cannot ride all night: we will need to seek shelter. Luckily I know a place, and if we ride fast enough we can reach there by sundown." She dropped back slightly to pull her horse in alongside Harriet's. They could ride two abreast now as they were the only two riders on this road as far as the eye could see.

The two women settled into companionable silence, the only sounds the clipping of hooves on the roadway and the occasional snort from one of the animals. They were not quite moving at a trot – it was more like a fast walk – and Harriet was content to remain at that pace. She finally had time to take in her surroundings, and was quite enjoying this little taste of the Italian countryside now that she didn't have impending disaster breathing down her neck. The open, rolling hills of green were dotted here and there with the imposing spire of a church or distant castle. There were rows carved into the green landscape, dotted with berries of all colours. Vineyards, overflowing with ripening grapes, scented the air as the two teenagers rode through the splendour of a summer day in Verona. The sun was hot, but it was a dry heat that Harriet wasn't used to. It was probably several degrees hotter than her native Australia, but there was no humidity that could make you feel like you were swimming, rather than walking. Sweat beaded on Harriet's skin as they rode, but it didn't settle and coat her like a dripping mantle of oppression. Harriet loved summers in Australia, but by God they could be brutal. She remembered the time that she had been branded with the seatbelt as she carelessly flung it over her shoulder without checking how hot it was. And the time that Mason's rubber thongs had melted when he'd left them out in the sun. Her little brother had gone shoeless for a week for his carelessness. He hadn't seemed to care though, and when he got bindies in his feet, he had cheerfully sat down to pull them out before taking off again to chase after Tristan. A wistful smile lit Harriet's face as she remembered her family. Having brothers was so uncomplicated, even if they could be annoying. She missed them desperately, as much as she was starting to enjoy her adventure now that she was away from the drama of Capulet Manor. She wished they could see what she could see, and experience a country that was so unlike their own.

The Italian summer was beautiful in its own right. They had seen no other travellers thus far, although they had ridden past a group of pickers working a grove of grapes near the roadway. They had smiled and inclined their heads, the men sweeping their hats off and bowing and the women dropping a curtsey. Apparently even this far out, Harriet's appearance on a horse was commanding enough to convince people she was someone of consequence.

She really needed to work on appearing more subservient. She had to fly under the radar.

The afternoon wore on as the two women plodded their way to their overnight refuge. Sometime around mid-afternoon, Caterina gauged the position of the sun and said, "It's no good, my Lady. We're going to have to move faster. We'll never reach the hut by sundown if we continue at this pace."

She urged her horse into a canter and Harriet panicked. She had little choice but to follow however, so she held on tight to the reins and prayed she could keep her seat. Caterina shifted fluidly into a gallop and Harriet's nerves went into overdrive. She couldn't do that. She'd never galloped a horse before, she'd fall off and break her neck. She swallowed nervously as she fell further behind her friend. Raspberry seemed to want to move faster, and Harriet sensed she was holding back because her rider was holding so tightly to the reins. Harriet eased her grip slightly and Raspberry sped up a little, maintaining the gap between the two riders. As Harriet remained upright, she eased her grip a little more and Raspberry shifted into a fluid stride that actually bounced Harriet around a little less than the trot had.

Before long, Harriet began to relax and trust in Raspberry. She became distracted and exhilarated by the feel of the wind through her hair. Somehow, it seemed longer since she had arrived in this time. Her long brown locks flew backwards from her face; pushed aside by the oncoming wind, they danced in the lively kick of air rushing past. The warm breeze on her face felt amazing. Harriet had avoided the hand mirrors in this time, afraid of what she might see. She already knew that her hair had changed slightly and her fingers seemed longer and thinner. Anything else Harriet simply didn't want to know about just yet.

Riding a horse was very different to travelling in a car. With the tinted windows rolled up and the air conditioning blasting, it was difficult to truly experience your surroundings. Not like this, anyway. She knew that her brothers would love this; Mason in particular. Although she was experiencing something truly incredible, deep down Harriet was anxious to return home, for the story to end. She wanted her normal, predictable life back, with the people that she loved in it.

Caterina suddenly whooped as her white cap flew off her head. She grabbed at it but missed, and it danced on the wind to land in the branches of a tree next to the road. She reined in Marmalade and the rampaging mare reluctantly obeyed her mistress. Harriet tightened her grip on the reins and hoped that was the way to slow a horse down. No one had talked about how to stop the damn thing! Raspberry responded to her light touch and slowed, but they missed the point where Caterina and Marmalade had halted by a noticeable distance. Not game to attempt turning the horse around, Harriet shifted in the saddle to watch Caterina pluck her cap from the tree and wheel her horse back to join her.

"It's been so long since I had a decent ride!" Caterina exclaimed, her blue eyes sparkling. Her face was flushed and her long blonde hair had come free from its binds, cascading down to reach her waist. Harriet wondered if all women in this time had princess hair. She was certain not all had hair as beautiful as this, though. It looked like spun gold and it curled slightly as it wended its way in a waterfall down Caterina's back. Harriet feared that Caterina would have more of a fight than she was expecting, if she chose to break with her family and reject the mysterious, repulsive Paolo.

"We've not got much further to ride," Caterina said, as she pointed to a hill in the distance. "The hut lies at the bottom of that hill, and it will not take us long to reach it. Which is just as well," she continued. "The sun will sink rapidly from here and we do not want to be travelling in the dark along these roads."

Caterina urged her horse on and Harriet fell in beside her, comfortable now in her command of Raspberry. Well, she wasn't actually sure that she really had command of Raspberry, but she was grateful for the patient and calm mare. As they rode, she stroked Raspberry's mane in silent thanks.

The shadows were falling as Caterina halted beside a grove of trees beside the road to Mantua. Harriet stopped as well, glancing around as she did so.

"Why have we stopped?" she asked, frowning. "It is getting dark, shouldn't we be continuing as fast as we can?" Harriet was beginning to get nervous about the deepening twilight. At first it had been magical, beautiful, but it also heralded the fall of deep night and Harriet wasn't too keen to ride on in the dark.

"We are here," Caterina said, smiling. She slid off Marmalade's back and grasped her reins. Harriet followed suit, patting Raspberry's nose as she stood at the horse's silky head. Caterina reached out and swept some low lying tree branches aside. Harriet could see a beaten earth pathway just beyond the edge of the road, leading away into the forest of trees. She swallowed nervously. Beyond the first bend of the track she couldn't see a thing.

"We'll have to go single file," Caterina said, motioning Harriet through the narrow entrance. Harriet sighed and began walking, leading Raspberry into the gathering darkness. The sound of the horse's hooves softened as she trod on the bare earth rather than the Roman cobblestones. Harriet's footsteps were also muffled and as Caterina swung the concealed entrance to the track shut, the silence closed in. Harriet's eyes adjusted to the dark as she moved forwards and around the corner. She passed two more bends before a small cottage stood ahead of her. It was basic and rustic, but it was a very welcome sight after hours of relentless travelling. It seemed familiar somehow, but Harriet couldn't put her finger on why.

Harriet led Raspberry into the wide opening in front of the cottage, taking in the small front porch of the cottage and the charming, hand built railing that lined the raised platform.

"This way," Caterina said, leading Marmalade to a smaller, ramshackle building near the cottage. It was a stable, big enough to fit four horses, and the women worked to get Raspberry and Marmalade into stalls. They removed their saddles – well, Caterina did – and brushed down each mare with straw. Leaving Caterina to settle buckets of oats in front of the horses, Harriet wandered out of the little hut and into the open clearing.

As she did, the door of the little cottage opened and a young woman emerged.

"Romeo!" she called excitedly. She stopped in her tracks. "You're not Romeo." She stared, her eyes widening. Harriet stared too, her mouth slightly open. Her own face stared back at her. This had to be Juliet.

Chapter Eight

"Well! What an afternoon!" Caterina said brightly, backing out of the stables and into the clearing. She turned, and halted. She stood stock still, taking in the scene in front of her. Harriet was standing near the hut, staring at the front porch of the cottage. Juliet was standing on the front porch, staring at Harriet. Caterina looked from one to the other. They looked almost exactly the same.

For Harriet and Juliet, it was like looking in a mirror. Sure, Juliet was dressed much more elegantly than Harriet currently was, but each woman possessed long chestnut hair, deep brown eyes and flawless skin. Each was captivating, and in the same room it was easy to see that each woman had a unique appeal of her own. Juliet had a weary worldliness about her – like she had seen too much in her short lifetime. In contrast, Harriet oozed the innocence of a sheltered and loving childhood. However, seeing the two separately, it would be difficult to tell the difference.

Caterina stood with her jaw dropped. What on earth was going on?

"Juliet?" she said, hesitantly. Both woman turned to look at her. Caterina's eyes widened and she backed away involuntarily.

"I'm Juliet, Cat," the woman on the porch said, her voice unsteady. "I have no idea who this is."

Harriet panicked. Caterina was looking at her like she was an alien, sent from somewhere she couldn't possibly understand. Well, that was sort of true, but that didn't make her an alien. She was as human as the two women in front of her, albeit an intensely modern one in comparison. Harriet knew this was the time to come clean. This was really her only chance of sorting this whole mess out and returning home.

She took an enormous breath, felt it swell in her chest, and she began.

"You're both going to need to keep an open mind."

Caterina and Juliet glanced at each other and by silent agreement, both moved to the bottom of the cottage steps. They were still several strides away from Harriet and seemed to want to keep it that way.

"Speak then," Juliet commanded. Harriet got a small glimpse of a spitfire, at odds with who she thought Juliet to be, before the controlled and demure young woman slipped back into place.

"Okay, I just need something first. It will help," Harriet said, her hands imploring the two women to stay as she dashed back into the stables. She hurried over to the brown case stored neatly against the wall of the stables. She unbuckled it and rummaged through it for the drawing she'd put inside as they had ridden through the afternoon. Sliding it free, she smoothed it down and looked at her own handiwork. What a mess it had led her into!

Harriet hurried back out into the clearing, clutching the paper to her chest. She approached Juliet and Caterina cautiously. The two were now sitting on a higher step, but from the rigidity of their spines Harriet could tell they were far from relaxed. She held out the page.

"This is the drawing that I made of Juliet…of myself…of something that was in my mind and needed to get out," Harriet began. The image looked like a blending of Juliet and Harriet, although Harriet's contribution to the drawing seemed to be fading away with each hour she spent in this time.

"Your story…in my time, it is a legend. Romeo and Juliet is a play, written by William Shakespeare. It follows the lives of two ill-fated lovers, Romeo and Juliet, who were forbidden to be together." Harriet saw a flicker of something in Juliet's face. She rushed on, committed to the truth now. "I was reading the story, playing around with the ending of it, and I fell asleep. When I woke, I was…here. In your bed, Juliet." she finished lamely.

Juliet was regarding Harriet steadily.

"Is that so?" Juliet appeared to be thinking steadily. "What does my bed chamber look like?" Mistrust rang in her tone.

"I found her in your bed chamber, Juliet," Caterina said quietly. Juliet turned her attention to her friend. "And you thought she was I?" Caterina nodded silently. Juliet turned to peruse Harriet again, noting the incredible similarities in their appearances.

She stood. "This story," she said. "How does it end, in your… legend?" Harriet did not want to answer that question. At least not yet. So she dodged it.

"I fell asleep with this picture under my pillow and when I woke up, I was in your bed…chamber at the Capulet Manor. I dropped in right before the ball celebrating your betrothal to Paris and I had to attend as you." Harriet paused, unsure of how to explain why she had poisoned Paris instead of herself. In for a penny, in for a pound. She closed her eyes briefly and then plunged straight in.

"I know your story, as Shakespeare wrote it. I've been able to tell what will happen next based on what I read. But…that's been a little harder since I began altering how each character acted. Well, mainly how you acted," she said, studying Juliet's face. It remained impassive. Harriet continued. "I knew that if I chose to take the potion, as you did in the original story, there was a very good chance the story would end the same way."

"And which way is that?" Juliet spoke in a measured tone, returning to her original question.

"You die," Harriet said simply. She didn't see any way around it. Who knew, maybe it would help. "Romeo does as well." Juliet sat back, clearly affected by this news. She looked up at Harriet.

"Prove it," she demanded. "Prove that you know this. How does he die?"

"Well, to be honest I was a little distracted when I read the ending," Harriet replied, encouraged by the fact that Juliet was talking.

She didn't want her to stop again, she didn't want to be shut out. She needed her to believe what was happening.

"From what I remember, Friar Lawrence gave you the potion." At Juliet's slight nod she continued. "In the original story, you take the potion after Romeo is banished to Mantua and your father forces you to marry Paris. Friar Lawrence sends a messenger to Romeo to tell him you are not dead; you will simply appear so until the potion wears off. But Romeo doesn't receive the message in time and he races to Verona. A text message would have saved all of that, but that's another story," Harriet offered a weak smile with her attempt at a joke. "He discovers you dead and he lays down next to you. He takes a vial of poison – I can't remember where he got that from, actually," Harriet frowned.

"Friar Lawrence," Juliet replied. "But continue. And then you will tell me what a text message is."

"Yes, well he takes the poison and as he dies, you wake up. You try to drink the poison too but it is empty, so you stab yourself to death with his dagger. Oh, and Romeo kills Paris too." Harriet finished her recount. "On the plus side, your deaths reunite your families and end the feud between the two houses." Harriet tried a tentative smile, unsure how that news would be received.

Juliet sat thoughtfully, staring unseeingly into the open clearing. She turned a ring over and over on her finger as she considered all that Harriet had said. Harriet could sense Juliet's restrained anger, though outwardly she seemed serene and calm. Harriet watched as Juliet's face gradually become stormy, as her thoughts churned over and over.

"So…you say that my husband will die. You have slept in my bed and acted in my place – the place of a noble woman." Harriet could hear the anger in Juliet's shaking voice. She was hanging onto her calm, but only by a thread. Harriet was beginning to glimpse the return of the spitfire.

"Wait, wait, wait," Caterina said, shaking her head as if to clear it. "If you're not Juliet, then who are you?"

"My name is Harriet Hunter," Harriet replied hurriedly, hoping that a change in the subject would circumvent Juliet's emotions. "I live in a country that has not been discovered yet. It will be called Australia, and my family lives in Tasmania. I have two brothers and my parents, and I'm really missing them. I want to go home, but I have no idea how to do that." Harriet appealed to the two young women, as old as she was herself. Her vulnerability showed in her face, as did her sorrow and longing for home. Just as Harriet could feel Juliet's anger pulsing across the clearing, Juliet could feel the sadness seeping from Harriet. She frowned at how clear the connection was between them.

Caterina stood up. Harriet watched warily, waiting to see how she would react. Caterina shook out her skirts and faced Harriet, bobbing her a curtesy. "It is a pleasure to meet you, Miss Harriet," she said, her lovely face serene and calm. Harriet couldn't quite believe it. But Caterina had more time to get to know her, and she could see that Harriet was no threat to them, at least outwardly.

Juliet got slowly to her feet as well, clearly struggling with something. She shook out her skirts too – the skirts of a gorgeous red and gold gown – and curtseyed.

"I'm not sure what the social protocol is for welcoming a maiden from another time and land," she mused, turning to Caterina. "I wonder if this is like the stories we are told in prayers, where Saints are sent to help those in dire need. It seems that Harriet is here at God's will, perhaps to help Romeo and I be together. There is no other explanation that makes sense. I hope this is the salvation we have been praying for." Harriet could see that Juliet was still struggling to come to terms with what was happening. Nevertheless, the training she had no doubt undertaken since birth in how to be socially graceful kicked in and took over.

"Welcome to Verona, maid Harriet." She tilted her head. "Are you of royalty in your own time?"

"Oh no," Harriet assured her quickly. "We don't really have royalty."

Juliet looked unconvinced. "No royalty. That seems strange. Tell us something else about your time."

Harriet went with the theme of the moment. "Well, there's still some royalty in the time that I come from, but they are nowhere near as powerful as now. There's Prince William and Harry of course, and their family I suppose. The royal family of England. But in Australia we don't have a King or Queen. We have a Prime Minister." Both women looked intrigued.

"A Prime…Minister?" Juliet said, rolling the words around in her mouth.

"They make the decisions for the country," Harriet offered. "It's a bit more complicated than that, but essentially they make the decisions. Like a King or Queen, I suppose, but they don't have absolute power and they're far less popular." Harriet smirked, thinking that was definitely true of Australia's current Prime Minister. "In fact," she said. "We've had our first female Australian Prime Minister. Things are different in our time," she continued, taking Juliet's unspoken invitation to sit down with the women on the stairs. She sank down onto the bottom step. She was aware that she had been chattering away, trying nervously to convince the two young women that she was genuine.

"And we aren't forced to marry men like Paolo," Harriet added.

"Are they still on about Paolo?" Juliet said, disgust written on her features. "Ugh. He is so far beneath you, Cat."

"I haven't had the pleasure of meeting the delightful Paolo," Harriet said. "But in my time, women choose who they want to marry. They marry for love. We can be anything we want to be, if we work hard enough for it. We have women doctors, lawyers, pilots, politicians, teachers and business leaders. Women are taken seriously; we have a voice. We can even vote for the person we want to represent us. Well, I can't. I'm still too young. But in two years I can, and I will."

Juliet and Caterina were hanging on Harriet's every word, their mouths slightly open. Harriet made a mental note to dial it back before she opened up questions she couldn't answer, or that would land her in hot water.

They were startled when a sound came from the opening of the clearing. All three looked up to see a man standing, a rabbit hanging from his hand. He was staring at the porch through the gloom, squinting through the gathering darkness to see who had joined Juliet. It was Harriet's turn to stare, open mouthed. It was definitely Romeo Montague who had entered the clearing, which explained Juliet's greeting earlier. Although she had altered Juliet's story, this was never part of the original as she knew it, and her changes could not possibly have created this situation.

Juliet confirmed it. "Romeo," she said, standing smoothly from her perch on the stairs. "Romeo, you must come and hear this." She hurried over to the young man and took his free hand, towing him back to the porch. Romeo's blonde hair glinted in the gloom as Juliet dragged him along. His clothes were well made and fashionable, although a little dusty and dirty. As Romeo got a better look at Harriet's face he did a double take. He looked from Juliet to Harriet and back again. Caterina let out a chuckle.

"Ha!" she chortled. "I imagine my face looked much the same way, Romeo," she chuckled. Romeo stood, dumbstruck. "But how…you two…you look…you're almost identical!" He spluttered. Juliet laughed.

"Yes, I too was a little surprised," she said. "It's dark, let's go inside and continue this conversation, shall we?" She was right. As they had spoken, night had fallen. The sound of chirping crickets filled the air and little rustles in the undergrowth announced the arrival of nocturnal animals. The four trooped inside and Harriet saw a tiny, threadbare cabin, sporting a small bed, two armchairs, a tattered rug and a banked fire. Juliet crossed to the fire and stoked it, throwing a few more logs on top to coax the fire back to life. As the flames began to leap, the room lightened considerably. Romeo began to set up a stick to use as a rotisserie for the rabbit.

Harriet felt anxious and unsettled. Romeo's appearance in the clearing had thrown her and she wasn't sure how this storyline was evolving now. It was unravelling out of her control, and Harriet felt an overwhelming need to get her feet back underneath her somehow.

"I wasn't expecting guests," he said apologetically, gesturing to the small animal.

"Never mind," Juliet said. "We'll make it stretch." As the smell of cooking filled the tiny room, Harriet's stomach grumbled. She hadn't realised just how hungry she was until she had smelled food. She'd never eaten rabbit, and she felt a bit queasy about doing so, but her stomach rumbled too greedily to be denied.

"Oh, we have some food out in the stables as well," Caterina remembered, starting up from the chair she'd settled into. Romeo stood up, and opened the door, accompanying Caterina to the stables. Harriet mused that there was something that struck her as unusual about this, but she couldn't put her finger on what it was. They came back moments later with the brown case and two extra canvas bags Caterina had carried on her horse throughout the afternoon. Harriet hadn't known it contained food too, and that was probably just as well. Her stomach growled with hunger. She hated to think what would have happened to her without Caterina. Taking off with a bag full of jewels and no way to convert that to money or food would have been foolish and dangerous. Hindsight was a wonderful thing.

"Would you like some water?" Juliet asked. "You must be parched." She filled two mugs and took them to Caterina and Harriet, before heading back to pour some for herself and Romeo. She noticed Harriet hesitating and said, "You don't need to fear this water, we boiled it after we collected it from the nearby stream. It's safe to drink."

Harriet didn't need further encouragement. She drank deeply from the mug, draining it in seconds. Juliet filled it again without comment. Caterina drank her fill as well, thirsty from the drama and effort of the day.

Romeo settled down on the rug beside the fire, turned the rabbit then focussed his attention on the ladies. Juliet sank down beside him and snuggled close to his side, and Caterina and Harriet sat in the two armchairs.

"So…care to fill me in?" Romeo asked.

"Would you like me to summarise?" Juliet asked Harriet. She nodded her consent.

"Harriet lives in…a land far from here. In another time. Somehow she's found herself in this one, in my bedchamber specifically. She arrived the day of the ball, the same day I fled here in the early hours of the morning. That might explain why we've not seen any signs of a chase yet," she mused. As Juliet spoke, a lightbulb exploded over Harriet's head. Juliet had already fled Capulet Manor. Perhaps THAT'S why she'd been sent to this time.

"Harriet attended the ball as me, pretending to be betrothed to Paris." She stopped and frowned. "Actually, that's all we got to. We know that Harriet is aware of how our story ends – or a version, anyway. It is written that we are ill fated lovers, who are destined never to be together. We both die in the version of our story that Harriet knows: you by poison and me by your dagger." She hurried to clarify as Romeo looked at her in horror. "Not by your hand, my love," she said. "By my own." She crossed herself, and so did Romeo and Caterina. Another epiphany for Harriet. Suicide was a big deal in this time, and was a much more shameful act that in was in her own. Families rejected those who took their own lives in this era, which explained why Escalus' man was so certain Paris wouldn't have taken his own life. Juliet was still speaking.

"I understand that I find you dead and I kill myself. Also, you've dispatched of Paris." She frowned. "That's a shame. I don't want to marry the man but I have nothing against him personally. He's actually rather nice."

Romeo spread his hands wide. "He won't die by my choice, my love," he said.

Juliet turned to Harriet. "What happened after the ball, Harriet? How did you come to be here, in this cabin with Caterina?"

Harriet settled herself comfortably in the chair. Caterina curled her legs under herself, her serviceable brown skirts draped over, spilling to the floor. She rested her head on her hand and watched Harriet explain.

All three sets of eyes stared as Harriet explained how she'd left Paris on his bed.

"But how did you get him to take the potion?" Caterina asked, her eyes wide.

"I snuck into his room and slipped it into his ale," Harriet admitted, hanging her head. Caterina and Juliet stared, then laughed with delight.

"You're jesting!" Juliet said, chuckling.

"I kid you not," Harriet said wryly.

"But how did you get into his room?" Caterina asked.

"I knocked on the door," Harriet replied.

"And you went in!" Caterina gasped. "In what must have been the dead of the night? That was a huge risk, Harriet!"

"It had to be done," Harriet replied. "Besides, why is it such a big risk?"

"You went into a man's room, uninvited, in the middle of the night! Anything could have happened!" Caterina exclaimed.

"To be honest, I was more worried about being seen," Harriet replied. "Not because of my reputation." She shot an apologetic look at Juliet, who shrugged it off. "But because I had a fair idea how this was going to end and I couldn't afford to be implicated in Paris' 'death'. So I slipped the potion into his ale and arranged it to look like he had poisoned himself. Friar Lawrence assures me there will be no ill effects from the potion, and the story I know supports that. But still I worry about him. He's a nice man." Harriet trailed off, feeling intensely guilty about what she had done. Paris would be lying in state now, his loved ones preparing to bury him.

"What happened next?" Romeo prompted.

Harriet explained how Nurse had caught onto what she had done, and had dressed her appropriately for an audience with Lord Capulet. Harriet paused, collecting her thoughts. She turned to face Juliet.

"You know, I get it," she said, gesturing to Romeo and Juliet. "I get why you thought there was no other option. He's really rather unbending, isn't he?" Juliet nodded. "But there has to be another way: there has to be a way that he'll come around to this." Harriet gestured to Juliet and Romeo. She continued. "I went straight back upstairs and I rang for

Nurse. But I got Caterina instead, and boy am I glad I did." Harriet smiled at Caterina, who returned her smile.

"Caterina…I wanted to tell you what was going on, I did. But I didn't know how you would take it or if you would help me if you knew who I really was."

"Oh don't worry on that," Caterina said, waving the apology away. "I would have acted in the same manner."

"You have acted in the same manner," Juliet said quietly, raising her eyebrows at Caterina. Her eyes took on a gleam of amusement. "Harriet, was Caterina in the story that you read?" Harriet shook her head.

"No, Caterina isn't in the original play," Harriet said. "She was unexpected, but luckily for me she was just the right person to come along at that time."

"You have no idea," Juliet said, a faint smile on her face. "Go on Cat, tell her who you are." Caterina looked nervous for the first time since Harriet had met her. She smoothed her skirts down and wove her fingers together before answering.

"Well," she began, nervously shifting in the armchair. Caterina paused, and instead of revealing her identify, she began to tell the story of how her parents had met. Caterina's mother, Margaret, wasn't from Italy, but was an Englishwoman. Caterina's father met her when she came to Italy with her own father on business. She was to be married to an English Baron, and her father was a Marquis in the English nobility. Margaret had been extraordinarily beautiful; which Harriet didn't doubt as she looked at Caterina's stunning face. Her father, Carlos, was a stable hand at the time, and he was in charge of the horses for the visiting party during their stay. He fell desperately in love with Margaret.

"My mother always said that as soon as she saw my father, she felt like she'd been hit by lightning. She knew that she loved him from the day she met him," Caterina said wistfully.

"But she also knew that she was about to be betrothed in marriage to another man, upon their return to England." Caterina's face darkened as her story continued.

Her parents begged Margaret's father to allow them to remain together, but he was furious at their union. He threatened to leave Margaret behind in Italy if she ever saw Carlos again.

"He broke her heart. My mother loved her father dearly, but had to follow her own heart. Her love for my father was strong, much like the love I see between these two," Caterina smiled, gesturing towards Romeo and Juliet.

"They met on her last night in Italy, and my mother made the choice to stay with my father: no matter what. It wasn't easy on either of them, and my grandfather was horrible about the entire thing. He left and my mother stayed, stranded in Italy."

Caterina's mother had slipped from a life of decadence and security to relative poverty and squalor. But to hear Caterina speak about her, she was always cheerful and loving to her husband and her children. Harriet's stomach twisted as she realised Caterina had been speaking about her mother in past tense. She watched as Caterina swallowed hard, impending dread filling her senses.

"When I was five, my mother got sick. She was fine when she woke, but by lunchtime she was dead. My father was devastated. He grieved for years, and to be honest, he still grieves now. His heart will never be whole again. I think that's why he isn't against me marrying Paolo," Caterina said, thoughtfully. "He knows that I don't love Paolo, and I suppose that's his way of attempting to protect my heart from being shattered, as his was – still is." Caterina refocused on the room, coming out of her reverie.

Despite Caterina's understanding of her father's motivations, Harriet was shocked. She couldn't comprehend how Carlos could do to his daughter what had been done to him in his own youth. But, despite Caterina's explanation about her heritage, she was still confused.

"So…let me get this straight. You are the daughter of English nobility, living in Italy as a maid?" Caterina nodded. "Have you tried to contact your grandfather?"

"I have nothing to say to a man who would leave his daughter in a foreign country to die," Caterina said passionately, her eyes flashing. "Besides…I know that I can get out of this myself, whether I'm noble or poor."

"It explains why you speak so elegantly," Harriet said, the realisation dawning on her. "And why Romeo helped you get the bags before, despite your position as a maid. So…do you outrank Juliet? Should I be curtseying to you?"

"Lord no," Caterina said with a laugh. She shot a mischievous look at Juliet. "Well, I would perhaps outrank her if my family recognised me. But they don't, and without that recognition a maid is all I can be. Besides," Caterina said, with a mischievous grin for Juliet. "The Italian nobility look down their noses at the English."

"That's the English who do that!" exclaimed Juliet indignantly. The two women laughed, their friendship and love for each other evident in the bond between them. Harriet was reminded of her own best friend, back in her own time. The bond between them was nowhere near as strong as that between Juliet and Caterina, and they had far less in common that this pair, despite the dramatic difference in their stations. Harriet pondered that as the fire spat sparks into the sparse room and the group sat in companionable silence.

Romeo stirred from his place on the floor and he turned the rabbit once more. "So as I see it," he said. "We now have Juliet and Harriet free. We have Caterina free from Paolo – thankfully."

"Alfonso will need to find another way to expand his business. I'm no pawn of his." Caterina was defiant.

"Alfie does what he must," Juliet chided Caterina gently.

"I know," Caterina sighed. "Sometimes it's easier to hate him though. He'll probably send me to a convent once this is all over." She laughed to lighten the mood. "Anyway, I'm free for now. He must be having a conniption."

"Yes, speaking of that," Romeo said, his frown becoming clearer. "Capulet will be looking for Juliet, who he will have realised is missing when neither of you showed up to the wake for Paris. Alfie and Carlos, and probably Paolo, will know that Caterina is missing. They won't have the resources to search for us, as Capulet does, but given the friendship between you two," he said, gesturing to Caterina and Juliet. "How long do you think it will be before they put two and two together? We have to act quickly. Aside from that, Paris is going to be buried in his family's vault if we don't act fast. Or worse, wake up in front of everyone and want answers, then and there. Harriet, does he know that you drugged him?"

Harriet nodded her head, apprehension clear in her expression. She had worried about that part. Romeo's face firmed.

"Right," he said. "I know Paris, and how he thinks. He plays by the rules…I don't. What would he do in this situation? Because whatever it is, we will be doing the opposite.

"We're in completely new territory," Harriet mused as she stared at the fire. "This," she waved her arm around to indicate the hut and everyone in it. "This doesn't happen in my version of the legend. I have no idea what will happen next."

Romeo's eyes gleamed wickedly in the light of the fire, and he took Juliet's hand and raised it to his lips. She blushed visibly. "Making things happen is what I do best," Romeo said. He jumped up and pulled their meal off the fire. "Leave it with me, ladies."

Harriet frowned – she'd rather be in charge of her own plan. But Juliet and Caterina were content to let Romeo think on it, so she tried to calm her nerves and step back long enough to see what he came up with. With Paris, Harriet had felt safe. Romeo was right, he did seem to play by the rules. It was not so with Romeo…she sensed that he was far more unpredictable than his love rival.

Harriet sat back, content for the moment to let Romeo's machinations out to play.

Chapter Nine

Harriet tossed and turned on the narrow strip of bed she occupied. She tried not to bump into Caterina as she flipped over, trying to get comfortable on the hard, thin bed. She cracked her eyes open and saw Juliet's serene face, firelight flicking over her features. She was peacefully sleeping in one of the armchairs, Romeo in the other beside her. How anyone could sleep in those chairs was beyond her. Romeo was trying, but he looked as uncomfortable as Harriet felt.

Harriet squeezed her eyes shut, knowing she'd need sleep to be sharp and alert before dawn broke over the horizon. It was around midnight, and they had a couple of hours left before they would head back to Verona. They were perhaps four, maybe three, hours hard ride from the city. The roads should be empty at that hour of the morning and the four fugitives were hoping to sneak back into Verona before the city woke from its slumber.

They would need all the cover they could get to sneak into the vault holding Paris.

Harriet went over the plan again in her head. They'd thrashed it out for hours, finally deciding to go with the simplest plan they could with the least potential for things to go wrong, despite Romeo's inclination to just bust in and grab Paris. They would all ride into Verona, two to a horse, leaving Star in the little paddock behind the hut here. She would happily remain, cropping grass and oats, waiting for Romeo and Juliet to retrieve her.

Harriet was pleased she'd be sharing a horse, given that they'd need to ride hard to make the city walls before daybreak. She would be much more confident riding behind someone else.

Romeo and Juliet were hoping to dissuade Paris from wanting to marry Juliet when he woke. They intended to throw themselves on his mercy; perhaps even tell him that they were already married, if it came to that. That had been the original plan, before Romeo's banishment and Capulet's ultimatum had forced them to flee. Juliet had been persuaded to run with Romeo, knowing that there was no way he would ever let them be together. Besides, it was unlikely her father would willingly give her an opportunity to speak with Paris privately prior to the wedding. But

Harriet's actions had shown Juliet that she could potentially be more decisive and confident, at least with Paris, and have some success.

Once they had dealt with Paris, Caterina was going to tell her father and brother that she would not marry Paolo. Juliet had offered to run interference on this and help Caterina stay out of reach of Paolo's wrath and her family's disappointment.

As for Harriet herself…after the story had been altered from its tragic ending, she would attempt to use the drawing again to get back home. Juliet was convinced that Harriet was a messenger from heaven, sent by God as an answer to her prayers. Harriet wasn't convinced – she wasn't overly religious – but she knew that Juliet's belief helped her to understand. It also helped to keep Harriet's neck off the chopping block.

Harriet thought that there must be a link between the way that Juliet looked and her almost identical appearance. Neither knew exactly what the link was between them, but both could feel that it was there; like a long, shimmering length of spider's silk.

Privately, Harriet wondered if Juliet was an ancestor, a long ago family connection she felt a particular affinity and closeness with. Now that they were in each other's orbits, the rapport between the two was developing rapidly and easily.

Harriet lay on her back, staring at the ceiling of the little hut. She couldn't sleep. Glancing sideways, she saw a cloud of blonde hair inches from her arm. In that cloud slept Caterina, her angelic face calm and serene. Even in her sleep, Caterina was an exceptionally beautiful young woman. The coming fight with Paolo about their betrothal was not going to be pretty. Harriet hoped she could help before she went back to her own time: she was starting to really like Caterina. She wanted her to be happy, to feel empowered to choose her own path. Harriet felt that Caterina had it in her to embrace a path of rebellion. She just needed a little encouragement to overcome the final hurdle and reach for a life of her own.

And Romeo, she mused as she stared upwards. He was interesting. Certainly a handsome young man, but not quite the sort of person she had envisaged. This Romeo was rebellious – a risk taker who went after what he wanted. He'd killed Tybalt, according to the original play, but Romeo vehemently denied it. When she'd asked earlier what they were going to do about Romeo's banishment, Juliet had said the only person who could lift it was Prince Escalus, Paris' kinsmen. She had explained that Escalus had banished Romeo without explanation, at least according to Capulet. Harriet puzzled over that inconsistency in her mind. Something was off there; it wasn't quite right. Why would Escalus banish Romeo for no reason? And if Romeo didn't kill Tybalt, who did? They were answers that would likely come out when they reached Verona, and Harriet was looking forward to finally having all the puzzle pieces she needed to form the complete picture.

Harriet looked over as she heard someone stirring near the fireplace. She watched as Juliet stretched and sat up straight, smoothing her hair back into its low bun. She yawned and looked over at the bed, straight into Harriet's face. She smiled.

"Can't rest?" she asked, her voice still carrying remnants of sleep. Harriet shook her head and swung her legs out of the bed, padding over to the rug in front of the fire. She was careful not to disturb Romeo as she settled closer to the light. Juliet shifted to sit beside her.

"It's odd isn't it," Juliet said, reaching out to touch the ends of Harriet's hair. "We look so alike, yet we're…how many years apart?"

"About five hundred, give or take," Harriet replied, staring into the flames. "Five centuries between your time and my time. I'm also half a world away from where you live – our homes couldn't be any more different. There are some similarities, but for the most part, it's different." Harriet sighed. "You know, the thing that bothers me the most is how you're treated; how Caterina's treated. No one would dare behave towards you in such a way if you were a man, and that's just wrong. In my time, it doesn't matter if you're a woman or a man. You're a human being and you have rights and entitlements, and you're allowed to have your own dreams, your own lives and to love freely. Marriage equality is even a thing now."

Juliet tilted her head to the side curiously. "What does that mean? Marriage equality?"

"It means people can marry whoever they want, whether they're male or female. Not every country recognises this, but it's something that's becoming more accepted around the world."

Juliet was intrigued. "That's amazing. Does Italy have...what was it? Equal marriage?"

"You know," Harriet said slowly. "I think that they just might."

Juliet's smile beamed from her face. "And women have the right to vote in Italy?"

"They sure do," Harriet said, infected by Juliet's happiness. But then she sobered "But these things didn't just happen, Juliet. People fought for them over generations and centuries. Women protested for their right to vote, all over the world. Many starved themselves and were imprisoned for speaking out about injustice. Some countries still treat women as second class citizens. Not Italy," Harriet said quickly, anticipating Juliet's next question.

"It's just all so surreal," Juliet mused, pulling her knees up underneath her chin. "These things are so foreign. It's impossible to imagine what it would be like to have such freedoms, to be able to do as we please, decide what we like."

"But it starts with you," Harriet said, turning to face Juliet. "It's not something that just happens overnight, it takes time. Men have become accustomed to women's rights and they've adjusted the way that they think. For the most part, anyway," Harriet said, frowning. "From what I've heard of Paolo, I'm not sure that he would evolve all that much."

Juliet wrinkled her pert nose. "Paolo is a beast," she said, disgust clear in her voice. "He wants Caterina as a prize, a trophy to dangle on his arm. She's an exceptionally beautiful young woman, and he knows where she comes from. But instead of celebrating how special and unique she is, he's used Caterina's background as a weapon. Coming from a union of love is one thing, but so is being disowned by your own family. In this time, the latter holds more weight. Those high up in Verona's society would shun Caterina and her family if they knew she came from a broken lineage who doesn't recognise her. It would be a life worse than being a servant." Juliet sighed. "I just want her to be happy. And I don't know how to protect her. I don't even know how to protect me."

"If we combine how I experience my world with how yours works, I'm sure we can find a way to get through this. It'll be challenging, sure. But we really have nothing to lose," Harriet said pensively.

"But you do, Harriet. We need to get you back to your time." Harriet sat silently, staring into the fire. She missed her family terribly, but there was work to do here. She had always been raised to step up and do what was right. Her mother was fierce and independent, but she was also kind, caring and sensitive when Harriet chose to see it. Some of that independence and fire had been passed down to Harriet, and she could use it to jumpstart Juliet and Caterina onto a new path. As she stared into the flames, she knew that her purpose was to provide that direction before she headed back to Wineglass Bay.

***

Two horses thundered through the still morning air. The crisp dew of summer had not yet settled on the grass and the pre-dawn countryside was grey and silent. Although it was relatively warm, steam was rising off the lathered horses. They were moving quickly, anxious to get back to Verona before the sun snuck over the horizon. If they didn't beat it, everything they'd worked for so far would likely be lost.

Harriet held onto Caterina as she manoeuvred Raspberry expertly across the terrain. Romeo and Juliet raced ahead on Marmalade. Caterina had told Harriet the night before that Raspberry was her father's horse and he would almost certainly be missing her. Although Carlos was ageing and didn't ride as much as he used to, he loved visiting with Raspberry and feeding her carrots. Caterina hadn't dared to touch her brother's stallion, Blackberry. She would have been discovered before they had left Verona with that proud beast.

The pre-dawn remained gloomy as the vineyards came into view, signalling that they had reached the outskirts of Verona. It wouldn't be long before the spires of the city would rise above the horizon. Harriet was grateful they weren't heading to Capulet Manor. She didn't think her nerves could handle creeping through the labyrinth of passageways and dank corridors again so soon. Before long, the steeples and hulking outlines of the buildings of Verona emerged from the shadows. They had agreed that once they got to the city centre they would need to leave the horses in a stabling house and head forward on foot. Four people cantering through the streets of Verona would raise significant attention, especially this early in the morning when only drunks and bakers were awake.

Caterina reined Marmalade in behind Raspberry and slid lithely down from her back. Harriet followed, less gracefully, but at least she kept her footing. As they walked the horses into a stabling inn, two sleepy boys came out to take their newest charges. With a nod, the horses were led away.

Harriet, Caterina, Juliet and Romeo slipped back into the streets of Verona, careful not to let their footsteps ring on the silent cobblestones. There was no street traffic to muffle their progress through the city, and they were careful to hug the shadows to avoid being seen. Their goal, the spire of the imposing Church of Sant'Anastasia, lay several streets away and they would have to cross open ground. Juliet had explained that inside the old and beautiful church they hoped to find Friar Lawrence and his Brothers, tending to Paris. Harriet was pretty certain that he would be at least beginning to wake, according to the calculations the Friar had given her. She was much lighter than the more muscular Paris and the dosage had been measured to drug her. Presumably, the potion wouldn't have affected Paris as long as it would have immobilised either Juliet or Harriet.

Splitting into pairs by silent agreement, Romeo and Juliet went ahead of Harriet and Caterina. This part of town was their domain, the play area of the rich and powerful. The architecture attested to that – imposing, awe-inspiring columns rose from the ground, supporting soaring ceilings with impossibly intricate stonework. Gargoyles and other mythical creatures decorated the facades of many buildings, each one more impressive than the last. Huge pointed arches soared over entry ways barred by impenetrable wooden doors studded with black metal.

The little band of friends stole through the alleys until they reached the open square they needed to cross. The wide staircase of the Sant'Anastasia was visible, leading up into its darkened entrance way. Even in the gloomy pre-drawn light Harriet could appreciate the beauty of the stonework adorning the entrance to the church. She didn't know what any of the technical names were for the parts of the building in front of her – she'd fallen asleep in the compulsory Graphics unit when the overly enthusiastic teacher had been talking about the difference between Gothic and Romanesque buildings. Although she might not be able to correctly label the building, she could see for herself its appeal and beauty. The entrance sported a soaring pointed arch with each layer recessed in towards the entrance way, like an accordion painted in alternating colours. It was captivating. Harriet tilted her head back and looked up to the topmost point of the church that she could see – the bell tower. It was huge and stood like a formidable guard protecting its city and people. She could just see the glint of a golden bell hanging in the open space created by pointed arch openings on the four sides of the square tower.

They needed to get inside before that bell tolled. It would signal the beginning of the day for Verona and already they could hear sounds of the city coming to life.

The Sant'Anastasia had two torches burning in brackets fixed to the wall beside the double doors. They illuminated the entrance way and made it impossible for anyone to approach the doors and remain covered by a cloak of darkness.

Harriet's attention was seized by Romeo, who had turned around with his finger to his lips. He motioned for the girls to come closer before he whispered, "There's a secret entrance at the back that will take us into the Friar's quarters. Lawrence took me there when he agreed to marry Juliet and I in secret. I know the way, but you have to follow me single file and don't lift your head, even if there's a noise. There is potential for people to see your face, especially in this light, and if you're taking the hidden entrance to see Lawrence, you don't want anyone to know who you are." Romeo crouched down low and pointed to a darkened strip along the side of the church. He motioned for the rest to follow.

Like four wraiths they stole through the shadows, keeping to the edge of the church and making sure their heads were down. Harriet had an overwhelming urge to look at everything she could possibly see, but she knew that Romeo's warning had been genuine. The last thing that they needed now was to be recognised. And two women together, who both looked like Juliet Capulet…well. That was something they didn't really want to attempt explaining.

The little group reached the back of the church unchallenged. Harriet snuck a glance around as Romeo approached the door, a miniature version of the grand front door. Instead of knocking, Romeo scratched the surface of the timber with his finger nails, in a repetitive and practiced pattern. His hand dropped to his side and he waited impatiently, exposed as he was in the gathering light as he stood on the threshold.

It felt like forever, but it couldn't have been long before the door cracked open silently. Its hinges were well cared for and they didn't make a sound in the still early morning, despite their age. Romeo gestured for them to follow as he pushed through the door, opening it only as far as he needed to get through. As Caterina slipped through the opening, the last of their group to gain the inside of the church, the door slid silently back into place and a bolt was pushed home with a metallic clunk.

The passage they were standing in was very narrow and its ceiling very low. Squashed as they were into the space, there wasn't much room to move. From her place between Caterina and Juliet, Harriet observed the Friar. Lawrence looked the same as he had when he had slipped into Juliet's room the night of the ball. His serviceable brown robes and sandalled feet, the rope around his waist and his tired eyes matched the memories Harriet had of the ageing monk. The Friar looked surprised to have four people standing in front of him.

"Romeo?" he asked, surprised. "What is going on? Where have you been? Juliet is missing! Nurse came to see me hours ago; she wanted to know if I knew anything. I'm beginning to think I have no idea what's actually going on here." The Friar stared as Juliet pushed the hood of her cloak back.

"Juliet!" the Friar exclaimed. "It is so good to see you hale and hearty…". The Friar broke off abruptly as Harriet stepped into the small circle of light thrown by the torch in the Friar's hand. Friar Lawrence looked from Harriet to

Juliet and back again. Then he whirled on Romeo.

"What is the meaning of this?" he hissed, his eyes wide in the gloomy darkness. "How…why…what is happening?" Friar Lawrence looked as if he'd seen a ghost. In the darkened hallway, the small similarities between Harriet and Juliet were muted, and the two did indeed look like carbon copies of each other. Harriet looked like Juliet playing at being a maid, and Caterina chuckled.

"Given your beliefs, Friar, I believe it would most likely be best if you didn't know the entire truth of what's happening here," Caterina suggested. "As you can see, having two people who look like Juliet allowed us to change our plans." Caterina smoothly explained as much as the Friar needed to know, with a nonchalant grace that made it seem as though she had been in on the whole charade.

"But I'm sure you've had enough of standing in this dank hallway, Friar Lawrence," Caterina said, taking the arm of the confused monk in a soothing motion. The Friar had begun to cough, a hacking bark that echoed through the cramped corridor. He was patently unwell, and although he was indeed of advanced years, his complexion reflected in the torch light and the rasping sound of his voice made him seem much older and more frail.

Caterina led Friar Lawrence away from the external door, walking unhurriedly with her arm linked through his. The Friar was too proud to lean on the young woman at his side for support, but it was obvious he could use some help. Romeo and Juliet followed in their wake, pulling Harriet along behind them.

They travelled through the chilly corridor, the walls damp and stony. It was hardly surprising to hear the Friar's rasping cough: he lived in such conditions. As he walked, the guiding light of his candle bobbed up and down, sending its feeble fingers into the shadows consuming their pathway. It seemed like there could never be enough flaming torches on the walls to touch the whole passageway; the light they had was struggling like a fledgling spark against the hunger of the dark. The swish of the monk's robes and the tap of their shoes on the stone floors were the only sounds that accompanied the Friar's laboured breathing. He stopped to rest, leaning against the wall of the corridor as he opened a plain wooden door and gestured the others through.

Harriet emerged into a room filled with light. It was so bright that her eyes stung as they adjusted to the sudden change. They were in a cavernous hall, the end closest to them ablaze with hundreds of candles. The sweet smell of a thousand flowers drifted through the air, tickling Harriet's nose as she sampled their sweet perfume. Awed, Harriet turned to look at every corner of the room. The far end was wreathed in darkness, the flickering candlelight sending shadows dancing on the brightly painted walls and ceiling. There were huge columns of red veined marble, spearing up from the floor to the high, vaulted roof. Heavy beams ran across, framing the frescos painted onto the plastered ceiling. Angels and babies, bearded men and beautiful ladies in flowing dresses filled the space above their heads. Window after window twinkled in the shifting light, the colours in the glass shining deep and true. Even the floor was a work of art, alternating between checked squares, geometric patterns and marbled elegance.

It was breathtakingly beautiful, and Harriet could have stared at it for hours without seeing everything in the room. But her gaze was drawn to the end of the long hall closest to where she stood. There was a nave, with two aisles leading up to it and row upon row of wooden benches marching back to the shadowy entrance, like soldiers lined up for battle. There was polished timber everywhere, and it glowed softly in the brilliant light of the candles.

Harriet's stare landed on a figure, laying silently on a brilliant white marble bench at the head of the nave. His arms were crossed over his chest and his face was tilted to the ceiling. He wore a resplendent blue and gold tunic and his boots shone darkly; polished and clean.

Paris. Her stomach churned with guilt as she watched him lay there, lifeless and motionless; essentially frozen in time. As she walked forward, approaching the shallow steps to the nave, Harriet could see Paris' dark hair shining in the flickering light of the candles. His face looked serene and at peace, exactly as it had the night she'd left him unconscious on his bed.

Harriet felt the air stir beside her. She glanced sideways and saw that Caterina had joined her and was staring down at Paris, an odd look on her face.

"I've only ever seen him from a distance before, and when I was meant to be working," Caterina said, a little breathlessly. She reached out a hand to touch his hair, hesitated, then let her hand drop without making contact. She folded her hands in front of her dress, linking her fingers together. "I've spoken with Juliet, of course, about Paris. But from the second she met Romeo she's been all about Montague." She rolled her eyes playfully. "Juliet never had time for Paris. But you know…he's a nice person. You can tell by the way that he treats his own servants. How does that work? I've never met the man, yet I feel like I know him." Caterina's expression was pensive. She reached out her hand again and this time, her fingers did connect with Paris' hair. She stroked the heavy locks back from his face, smoothing them into place.

Now that Harriet wasn't distracted by impending doom and disaster, she had time to look at Paris' face appraisingly. He really was quite an attractive young man, and she thought he would only grow to be more so with time. He didn't make Harriet feel anything – unless you counted gut churning guilt – but she could see that Caterina was affected by the nobleman's appearance. Harriet smiled a little to herself. So the wheel turned again. There may be some more complications to this story as they went along, happy complications.

Harriet swung away from the prone body of Paris as Romeo spoke.

"How is he not yet awake, Friar?" Romeo asked, his tone clearly perplexed. "The potion would be wearing off Juliet by tonight, and she's much smaller than Paris."

"Ah," said the old Friar. "Yes she is, but the potion was also formulated for a woman. There is a different recipe if the intended is a man."

Harriet looked at the old monk in horror. "You mean…I might have hurt him?"

Friar Lawrence hurried to reassure her. "No, my child," he said. "We are certain that Paris will wake in time; but we know not how much time it will take. We are anxious for him to wake, as Escalus will be here at daybreak to move his body to the family vault." As he was speaking, the monk had climbed the steps to the nave with painful, slow movements. He peered into Paris' face, contemplating the silent, unmoving man.

"We need to give him a little…jump start, if you will," Friar Lawrence said, moving around to the back of the nave behind Paris.

"And what does that entail, exactly?" Juliet asked.

"I'm unsure," the Friar admitted, rubbing his hands over his eyes. "We've never accidentally given the wrong potion before. At least, not one that someone has lived through," he amended. They all stared at that. Friar Lawrence waved a hand. "But that's not important now," he said hastily, as the first rays of the sun burst through the stained glass window behind his head, shooting rainbow shards of light around the hall.

"Harriet," Juliet said pensively. "Is there anything at all –," she lowered her voice. "Anything from your time that might help us here?"

Harriet tried frantically to marshal her wits sufficiently to answer the question. Modern medicine wasn't going to help here. She didn't really know enough about it, and it wasn't like they had an arsenal of tools and medications at their disposal. The treatments here were primitive, mostly natural herbs and remedies, and in this case that would hardly be effective. Besides, the monks would have already tried it anyway.

"Something from another story you've heard, perhaps?" asked Caterina, trying to prompt some idea out of Harriet.

She considered that. She thought about the types of stories she knew. Shakespeare – her knowledge was limited. The Babysitters Club. Well…that was unlikely to be useful here. Children's stories, fairy tales, Disney movies…fairy tales. Harriet's spinning mind flicked back as a harebrained idea began to take shape. It was ridiculous, but then so was the concept of her travelling back in time and appearing identical to a 14th century noblewoman. Nothing about this situation was normal or logical, and so far she had succeeded by trusting her gut feelings. Harriet took a risk.

"Do you have fairy tales here?" Harriet asked.

"Do you mean like folk stories and fables?" Juliet asked, frowning slightly. "Like…stories that we're told as children?"

"Yes!" Harriet exclaimed. "Yes, exactly! Which ones do you know?"

Juliet frowned, and so did Caterina. "Well…there's one about a blacksmith and the Devil," Caterina mused. "Well now that's ironic really, isn't it?" she said with a chuckle. Harriet and Juliet joined in.

"How did that story go again?" Caterina asked Juliet.

Romeo replied. "The blacksmith traded his soul for the ability to weld any materials together. Then when he gained his new power, he stuck the Devil to a tree so that he couldn't take his prize: the blacksmith's soul. However, the Devil tricked a passer-by into releasing him in exchange for the blacksmith's forge. The man did as the Devil asked and the demon was freed. He took the blacksmith's soul and condemned him to eternal damnation for attempting to trick the ruler of the underworld out of his rightful property.

It's a childhood story, and one that I enjoyed so I remember most of it. The moral is to always be true to your word. My father drummed that into us when we were kids, my cousins and I."

"Sounds like something Paolo would do," Caterina chortled. "If he would make a pact with the devil it would save me a lot of trouble!"

Harriet stared. "Wow," she said, her eyes wide. "Your fairy tales are intense! Ours are more about princes and princesses, who turn into magical creatures and need true love's kiss to break the enchantment and become human again. Some are turned into bears, or beasts — some are poisoned with potions that make them appear dead…," she trailed off, her gaze snapping up sharply. A ripple of understanding passed between the four.

"But…," Juliet said, frowning. "If that is going to work for Paris…who is his true love? Who will kiss him? I'm certain it is not me."

"Well," Harriet said, grimacing. "He might think that it is you, and perhaps that will be enough? I'm not really sure what happens if one of the pair doesn't love the other. In the fairy tales, the prince and princess always love each other, even if they don't know each other well. It's really rather far-fetched, but they're fabulous stories for little children."

Juliet glanced at Romeo, who nodded slightly. "We've put poor Paris through quite a bit, pursuing our love. I suppose it's only right that I should try. What do I do?"

"True love's kiss, Juliet," Harriet said. "You have to kiss the boy. Right here," she said, tapping her lips with a teasing smile.

"I don't see why you can't do it," Juliet hesitated. "I hope he doesn't get the wrong idea." She stepped quickly up to Paris before she lost her nerve. Swooping down, she touched her lips to Paris'. Nothing happened. Not so much as a hair stirred on Paris' head. She tried again, this time lingering just a tiny bit longer. Still nothing. Juliet made an exasperated noise and looked at the others.

"Sorry," she mumbled guiltily, moving back to stand with Romeo. He rubbed her back in consolation. Friar Lawrence threw up his hands.

"This is hocus pocus that I know nothing of," he said stiffly. "Don't look to me for answers."

Juliet looked at Harriet. "What now?" she asked, glancing up at the window above the pulpit that was showing a new day well and truly beginning to emerge. "We don't have much time left."

"Let me try," said Harriet, shrugging slightly. She stepped up to Paris and touched her lips to his, as Juliet had done. She hadn't really expected it to work, but she was still a little disappointed as Paris continued to lay motionless on the cold marble slab.

"Well, I'm not having a go," Romeo said, a smile quirking his lips. "I don't think a girl-stealing Montague is really his type." Juliet put a reassuring hand on his arm. She didn't need to speak – her soothing message was communicated in her touch alone.

Harriet looked at Caterina. "Cat…you're the last one left. It's a long shot, but maybe…you could try, anyway. Better start thinking of a Plan B," Harriet said to Romeo and Juliet, who nodded their understanding.

Caterina moved slowly back to Paris' side, her eyes fixed on his face. It was clear she was nervous, and Harriet wondered if this was her first kiss. She thought women were married young in these times, but then Caterina had made no secret of the fact that she found her intended husband repugnant. She'd hardly be in a rush to kiss him.

The candlelight flickered on Caterina's striking face as she swept her long blonde hair out of the way and over her shoulder. It had escaped its confines on the road back to Verona and she hadn't had time to smooth it back properly. Harriet was envious that Caterina still looked perfect, while she looked as though she'd been dragged backwards through a bush.

Caterina leant down to Paris, hesitating just as her lips were about to touch his. She steeled herself and closed the last inch, touching her lips to Paris'. There was a blast of air and Caterina's hair flew back from her face, then danced slowly back down to rest on her back. She looked at the others, surprised. Then she let out a startled squeak as someone touched her hand.

Caterina looked down to see Paris' eyes were open, and he was regarding her steadily. She could see that they were a dark brown colour, very deep and intense. His hand was gripping hers lightly, and she watched as he squeezed her hand gently.

"What has happened?" Paris asked, disoriented and confused. He went to sit up, but a wave of dizziness hit him and he slumped back down onto the cold marble. Romeo rushed to fill a cup with water, and he handed it to Caterina to urge on Paris. Caterina supported his head as he drank deeply. When he'd had his fill, she returned his head gently to the marble pillow. He grimaced, turning his head this way and that to ease the cramp in his neck. Paris turned to the side and caught sight of Harriet. Abruptly, his expression darkened and he struggled again to sit upright.

"You!" He said, his eyes widening. "You did this! You POISONED me!" Paris' tone was outraged, his face flushing with colour. "Why, Juliet?" Paris' attention was captured by a small movement, and he saw the couple standing just behind and to the side of Harriet. He stared, then shook his head as if to clear it. "I'm hallucinating," he said, shaking his head more vigorously when both women remained in his vision. "What did you give me, witch?" He demanded. Harriet winced. There was the word she'd been afraid of. Juliet stepped forward to stand beside Harriet and took her hand in support. Paris' eyes flickered from one to the other, but he no longer shook his head. "Paris, I am Juliet," Juliet said, holding her other hand out imploringly. "And we have a story to tell you. But just now I'm in danger – we're all in danger," she corrected. Glancing up at the window, she estimated that it wouldn't be long before Prince Escalus came to retrieve the body of his kinsman. "Will you trust us?" Juliet asked imploringly. "I promise you, we will tell you everything."

Paris looked from Juliet to Harriet, to Caterina before his gaze landed on Romeo. He narrowed his eyes. "Montague," he said, animosity clear in his voice. The faint sound of horses moving through the streets filtered up to the nave of the church.

"Paris," Romeo replied steadily, refusing to be drawn.

"Paris, please. Will you trust us?" Juliet's voice rose urgently as the thunder of horse's hooves became louder. It sounded like an army of people were about to descend on the grand church. The shadows were receding and the room was flooding with daylight, enhanced by the guttering candles that were still burning.

Paris weighed his options. He regarded Juliet – at least, the one who said she was Juliet – and said, "What do I have to do?"

Juliet breathed a sigh of relief. "Come with us, to the catacombs under the church," she said quickly. "We will explain everything there. We must not be discovered here. If you want to leave after we explain, no one will stop you." Romeo looked like he might be about to contradict his wife's words, but a swift glance from his beloved silenced his tongue.

Paris locked eyes with Juliet, trying to determine if there was truth or trickery in what she was saying. She held his gaze steadily, refusing to show any weakness. It was imperative they all get to the catacombs urgently.

"Fine," Paris said, hauling himself upright and swinging his legs over the edge of the marble dais. He grimaced as blood flowed back into his limbs, unused for over a day. Romeo instinctively caught him as he tumbled from the dais, balancing his weight and flinging one of Paris' arms over his shoulder. Caterina hurried to Paris' other side and slung his free arm behind her neck, helping him to stand and walk upright. Harriet and Juliet raced to swing open the door to the back corridor, the darkness beckoning to them once more.

"Of course," Friar Lawrence muttered, as a booming knock sounded at the bolted church doors. "Leave me here to deal with Escalus. What will I tell him? This is madness, I tell you, madness." His voice trailed away as he slowly shuffled down one of the long aisles to unbolt the heavy door.

Harriet swung the internal door shut as Romeo, Paris and Caterina limped sideways through it. She breathed a sigh of relief at their timely escape.

They had to put their faith in the Friar now. He had to give them enough time to convince Paris, to show him that his future was not with Juliet.

Chapter Ten

"What do you mean, he's gone?" Prince Escalus demanded, his voice booming up to shake the top rafters of the vaulted ceiling.

"Well, you see my Lord," Friar Lawrence said with unruffled calm. "The undertakers arrived at daybreak this morning, just as you said they would, and they took young Paris off to your tomb. Is that not what you requested?" Friar Lawrence was exceptional at dissembling.

Escalus frowned. He turned to his most trusted advisor, who was standing beside him with his hand on his sword hilt. "Is that what I asked, Matteo?"

Matteo shifted his hand from its menacing position. "I was under the impression we were taking him with us, my Lord, but it's entirely possible that Capulet arranged for the undertaker to remove Paris's body with dignity. Perhaps to make amends for his accusations against you yesterday?"

The Friar wasn't slow of mind. "Yes," he said, his face completely serious. "Now that you mention it, they appeared to be Capulet's men here this morning, helping to remove the body with dignity and ceremony. They were very respectful. I imagine that you didn't miss them by a great deal, my Lord," Friar Lawrence continued, lying point blank to Escalus' face. "They should arrive at the tomb before too long."

Escalus swept his gaze up and down the ageing monk and nodded, his face set. "Very well, good Friar," he said, motioning for his men to quit the church. Escalus followed his guards out with one last look around the splendid walls, a faint frown still shadowing his intelligent brown eyes. It wasn't often that he forgot something, and it wasn't all that common for him to misunderstand what was happening.

Escalus left the Sant'Anastasia with a slightly uneasy feeling. If something was wrong, he wouldn't stop until he found out what it was.

***

The little company hobbled through the damp tunnels as fast as Paris' legs would carry him. The blood had finally reached his toes, yet his legs were still weak and waves of dizziness crashed over him if he ducked his head and looked up again. They followed the passageway past the back entrance and onwards into the gloom. They'd twisted and turned, racing down the pitch black opening that seemed to go deeper and deeper into the earth. The floor was slanted slightly downwards, steeper in some places. The procession moved in single file, except for Paris and Caterina. She was small enough to fit beside Paris in the cramped hallways, unlike Romeo. He was walking on his own now, but Caterina stayed close in case he stumbled and Romeo walked slightly ahead as a second support.

Finally, the hallway opened up into a slightly larger, completely round room. It was totally bare; it contained absolutely nothing except more of the same floor and walls. However, there was a very faint light that shone down into the room, as if there were cracks in the ceiling here and there allowing it through. They could see that there were three other tunnels branching out of the round room, not including the one they'd come down.

"Stay there," Romeo commanded Paris and Caterina as he inspected each of the tunnels in turn.

"I can't see a thing down any of them, but at least we know we came down that one. That will be useful to know if we take the wrong tunnel." Paris nodded his agreement. Harriet thought for a second, then turned to Juliet. She removed the scarf from around Juliet's neck and tucked it into a ledge in the wall beside the opening where Caterina stood.

"Hansel and Gretel style," Harriet said with a grin. The others stared at her. "You know…brother and sister leave breadcrumbs to find their way back home from the witch's cottage? No? Never mind." Harriet made sure the scarf was secure before Paris and Caterina stepped into the round room.

"So…how do we decide which way to go?" Juliet asked. "And where do these tunnels go, anyway?"

Romeo was testing the last corridor. "These are the catacombs under the church. Some of the boys at our stables tell stories about being down here when they were small. One of these tunnels leads to the river, and another to the catacombs under another church. I have no idea where the third goes."

"Which one do we want?" Paris asked, his voice a rasping rumble after being silent for so long.

"The one that leads to the river," Romeo said. "It isn't too long and it will bring us out under this side of the Pons Marmoreus and the Ponte Pietra. The Escalus crypts aren't far from the Montague tombs, and both are down near the bridges to the theatre district."

"So…how do we decide?" Caterina asked, peering into the inky black hole that was the closest tunnel. She shivered involuntarily.

"All we can do is try them, one after the other." Romeo said simply, shrugging his shoulders. "And pray we choose the right one first, because time is running out for us to sort this out. We have no idea what Friar Lawrence said to Escalus, but it will only hold him for so long. Eventually they'll realise that Paris' body is not where it's meant to be."

"Wait," Paris said, frowning. "We came down here because you wanted time to explain to me what happened. Why can't you just explain here?" It was clear that Paris would have preferred the option to go back in the direction they had come from if he didn't like what Romeo and Juliet had to say. The two glanced at each other, silently debating their options. In the end, Caterina decided it for them.

"Actually," she said with a small shiver. "If we could take one of these tunnels out into open air before we talk at length I'd be very grateful. I'm not overly keen on enclosed spaces."

Paris regarded her steadily before he said, "Okay. I'll wait until we reach the other end. Which one?" He paced across the small room to stand in front of the central passageway. "I suggest this one." He looked back to the others, seeking consent or dissention. The rest shrugged – each option was as good a choice as the other.

The five of them set off down the darkened corridor. It was pitch black just a few paces in and they were forced to feel their way along the slime covered walls. Caterina's harsh breathing was very audible in the small space – it was clear that she wasn't enjoying this experience at all. Neither were the others, but Caterina sounded dangerously close to panicking. Harriet was behind Caterina – or at least she thought she was based on how close her breathing sounded.

"It's okay, Cat," Harriet said, trying to sound cheerful and unconcerned. "It can't be too much further now." She tried to lay her hand on Caterina's shoulder in the pitch darkness.

"That's not Caterina," came a low, rumbling voice. Harriet snatched her hand away. She was glad of the lack of light, so no one could see her flaming cheeks.

"She's in front of me," Paris said, his voice echoing again in the dark. Paris himself reached out to put a comforting hand on Caterina's shoulder. It pulled at his heartstrings to hear how frightened she was. As he touched her shoulder tentatively, Caterina reached back and clasped his hand a little desperately. Her breathing gradually steadied, so Paris stayed as he was, his hand sandwiched between her shoulder and her warm fingers.

They continued on like that for another two hundred paces, the slime on the walls thick with centuries of muck. Harriet felt like her hands would never be clean again and she made a conscious effort not to put them to her face for any reason.

Their eyes slowly adjusted as, by painfully slow increments, the unrelenting black of the tunnel gave way to the joy of sunlight. Romeo whooped as he moved faster into the bright disc that had appeared at what must be the end of the tunnel. The others moved more slowly, allowing the dots to mostly disappear from their eyes before they rushed ahead.

All five emerged into the clean air of the banks beside the Adige River, shaking the last of the fuzziness from their vision as they squinted against the bright, early morning sunshine.

Romeo flopped down on the sloping bank, turning his face to the open sky. The other four followed suit, breathing the fresh, salty breeze into their lungs and clearing away the cobwebs of ancient, stale air.

Harriet noticed that Paris and Caterina had still not left each other's side. Caterina seemed recovered, and indeed re-energised, by her emergence back into the living world. Her blue eyes sparkled as she stood daintily near the riverbank. Romeo and Juliet had plopped down together on the grassy bank, their closeness evidence of the special nature of their relationship. They were one of those couples who looked like they were two halves of a whole – as if on their own they just wouldn't be as complete. But they also looked slightly nervous, and Harriet supposed that was unsurprising. Their fate rested largely in the hands of the man in front of them – he who had been drugged and essentially kidnapped in the pursuit of their happiness. If Paris agreed to support their union, they could stand up to their families, confident in the support of the Escalus clan. But if he didn't…well, the course of true love was not destined to run smoothly.

Chapter Eleven

Harriet wondered how the couple were going to broach the topic, and was surprised when Juliet simply jumped straight in. Since the night before, Harriet could see the beginnings of a much more confident and straightforward Juliet. The difference between the Juliet she knew from the play and the Juliet before her now was even more pronounced. Harriet mused that the mismatch in information was a little like reading a secondary textbook…the facts were there, but sometimes it was easy for things to get lost or missed in the re-telling. A simple game of Chinese whispers showed just how easily a story could be skewed, and Harriet suspected that Shakespeare's version of Romeo and Juliet was not completely accurate. Nevertheless, a noticeable change had occurred within Juliet and part of Harriet hoped that she'd had some influence on the woman who looked almost identical to her.

"Paris," Juliet began, pressing her hands together. "I know that we are betrothed to be married, and I believe that you have wanted to marry me for some time." She took a deep breath. "You need to know…Romeo and I are already married." She scanned Paris' face for a reaction. He was frowning. She rushed on. "Neither of us intended our marriage as a disrespect to you, my Lord. We met and we fell in love on the spot. I know it sounds ridiculous, fanciful even, but I promise you it's the truth. I've never felt about anyone the way I do about Romeo. I cannot live without him, and I don't want to try.

I know that we have little right to ask this of you, given this isn't your fight and you've already been disrespected, even unwittingly, by us. But we need your help, Paris. Our families will be livid when they find out we've married without their consent, especially my father. And he'll be concerned, too, about the disrespect I've shown to the Escalus clan.

But you can help us," Juliet said earnestly, appealing to Paris. "We could come to some sort of agreement, perhaps, about our betrothal…" Juliet trailed off, trying not to babble. She lapsed into silence as she watched Paris absorb the new information. Romeo put a comforting hand on her back, silently soothing her nerves. Their future rested on Paris' decision. Oh, they intended to be together, regardless of his response, but it would certainly be easier if he agreed to help. There was no way Romeo could stay in Verona without Escalus' support, and to get that they needed Paris on board.

Paris was looking pensive. He hadn't yet spoken and didn't look like he intended to any time soon. He was clearly considering what Juliet had said. Uncomfortable with the silence, Juliet went to open her mouth again, but closed it when Harriet shook her head slightly from behind Paris' shoulder.

Then Harriet spoke. "Cat, Juliet. I'm going down to get a drink from the river." She stood and brushed off her now dusty brown skirt. "Come with me." Her tone suggested that they not argue and her words were firm. Both Juliet and Caterina received the silent message, rose without hesitation and fell in with Harriet as she turned to stroll a little way down the riverbank. The two men were left on the grass – one a handsome young man, long legs sprawled outwards with fair hair that glowed in the bright sunshine, the other sitting more stiffly, darkly good looking with striking features and colouring. Both looked faintly surprised, and not a little uncomfortable, to have been so summarily deserted by the ladies. Harriet marched to the water's edge.

"You aren't going to actually drink it, are you Harriet?" Juliet asked. Harriet remembered that in these times water could equal death, and she snatched her hands away from the river, folding them together in front of her skirt.

 "No. No I wasn't," she said. She had thought about it. She looked the two ladies straight in the eye, one after the other.

"That was a pretty speech Juliet," Harriet said. "I understand that you need Paris on board, but you also need to stand your ground. Don't get me wrong, you're much more assertive than the play I read would lead anyone to believe. But you're still deferring to a man to make your decisions. You need to tell Paris what *you* want! *I* still don't know what you want. All I know from what you've said is that you love Romeo and you're sorry you dumped Paris. Then you look at him like you want him to fix…whatever it is you want him to fix. It's a little hard for the poor guy to decide whether he'll help you if he doesn't know what he's helping with!

And you, Cat!" Caterina looked at Harriet in surprise. She had been nodding along with what Harriet had said. "Me?" she asked. "What did I do?"

"It's what you haven't done!" Harriet replied, exasperated. "Anyone with eyes can see that you are majorly interested in Paris." Caterina's face flamed red. "Tell him!"

Both Caterina and Juliet's eyes flew wide. "It…it doesn't work like that here," Caterina stammered.

"Oh really?" Harriet replied, her hands going to her hips in a gesture reminiscent of her own mother. "Then how did Romeo and Juliet defy their families and marry each other within what – two days of meeting?" Harriet looked to Juliet for confirmation. She nodded. Harriet turned back to Caterina with a smug expression. "There, you see! I bet Juliet didn't hide behind her manners, waiting for Romeo to come to her and declare his love. Isn't that right, Juliet?" Juliet was silent. Harriet looked at her and did a double take. "Oh come on! Is that what happened?" Juliet nodded, and Harriet made a sound of disgust.

"Ladies," she said, trying to keep her patience. "You don't always have to take your orders from a man. Cat, I expected better from you. Do you want to marry Paolo?" Caterina shook her head vehemently.

"I will never marry Paolo," she declared, her chin firming. "Even if I die instead, I will never marry that pig of a man."

"There's no need to be so dramatic about it," Harriet said, rolling her eyes good naturedly. "You need to be assertive and firm. It seems to me that Paris is the key to more than one of our problems." Caterina coloured again.

"You need to tell Paris that you…what do you say here?" Harriet asked, stumped. In her time if she liked a boy she'd simply tell him so. So would all of her friends. Sure, they'd squeal about it for a bit first before they worked up the courage to talk to them, but they went after what they wanted.

"We…well, usually we'd court?" Caterina said, looking to Juliet for confirmation. She nodded. "But that's initiated by the gentlemen, not by the ladies," Caterina finished. Harriet simply stared at her.

"And where did that almost get Juliet?" Harriet said steadily. "She nearly ended up married to the wrong man, and in turn that would have affected you. Anyone can see that you and Paris are wonderful together. Sure, he's just woken up from a day of being drugged and is probably still a little woozy, but I don't think that he's immune to you either, Cat. What do you have to lose by giving it a shot? The alternatives are marrying Paolo, fleeing the country or death, so how much worse could this be?"

Caterina nodded slowly. "Well, when you put it like that it doesn't seem like such a bad thing to do," she agreed. Then she became flustered. "What will I say to him? How will I say it? Oh," she said crossly. "There's a reason why ladies don't do this sort of thing!"

"Rubbish!" Harriet said. "They're as nervous as you are. Just give him a chance, you've got nothing to lose. Except time. We can't lose any more time. It's only a matter of it before Escalus launches a full scale hunt for Paris, and we certainly can't afford to be caught with him. At least not until we have his loyalty." They began walking back up the hill to Paris and Romeo, who were sitting uncomfortably, watching the river. They had spoken only occasionally since the women had been gone. Paris had been watching Caterina, trying not to be too overt about it. Romeo hadn't cared. He had eyes for only Juliet, and he had tracked her movements to the edge of the water and back. He rose as the ladies approached, and Paris followed suit.

"So," Caterina said brightly. "Where do we go from here?"

"First," Juliet said, marshalling her courage. "Paris. I need to explain myself further." Romeo stepped forward to stand with Juliet, but she motioned him back. Juliet glanced at Harriet, who nodded encouragingly.

"Paris, I want to be with Romeo. He is the man I want to spend the rest of my life with. We can't do that without your help – at least, not in Verona. Romeo was banished from the city, because he was accused of killing my cousin, Tybalt. But there was no way he could have, because he was with me when Tybalt died." Juliet's cheeks flamed, but she pushed on determinedly. "My father pushed for Romeo to be banished so he would be out of the way, leaving me free to marry you. He won't back down easily. We need your help to clear Romeo's name and to force my father's hand in agreeing to our union. The only way we can see that happening is if you go to Escalus, your kinsman, and tell him that you accept our betrothal will not go ahead and that Romeo is innocent. Friar Lawrence will attest to the fact that we were in the middle of our wedding ceremony when Tybalt was killed. I am prepared for the consequences if it means I remain with Romeo." Juliet raised her chin, staring straight into Paris' eyes. Harriet could see that while she seemed calm on the outside, her hands were tucked into the folds of her dress so that no one would see them shaking. She silently applauded her friend.

Paris looked from Juliet to Harriet and back again. "I have some questions," he said. "Which one of you attended the betrothal ball?" Harriet raised her hand slightly. Paris nodded. "And who drugged me?" Harriet motioned to herself again, her expression showing chagrin and guilt.

"If I may," Harriet interjected. "I am very sorry for giving you the potion, Paris. I'm glad that we got to you before your body was removed, and before you woke up without anyone there. How you woke up is another matter," she said, frowning. "We haven't really digested that just yet. But it makes me even more glad that things worked out as they did, or Caterina wouldn't have been with us and perhaps we wouldn't have been able to wake you. But I am sorry."

Paris frowned. "But…where did you come from? And who are you?" In their haste to escape the tunnels, they had forgotten that no one had actually told Paris who Harriet was. Romeo, Juliet, Caterina and Harriet glanced at each other, then Harriet shrugged. She had persuaded Juliet and Caterina to take a risk, the least she could do was show them how it was done. Harriet reached inside her sleeve and untucked the creased paper that contained her drawing. She smoothed it out against her skirt and offered it to Paris. He took the paper and poured over the lines of the face it contained, intrigued.

"This looks like a combination of you both," Paris mused. "There are some slight differences if you look closely enough."

"My name is Harriet Hunter," Harriet said, twisting her fingers as nerves assailed her belly. She crossed her fingers and prayed this went well. "I live in a time five hundred years from now."

Paris raised his head sharply. His eyes bore into Harriet's.

"Pardon me," he said politely. "Five hundred years from now?"

"To be honest, we don't really know how I came to be here," Harriet said truthfully. "I drew this picture after we studied the play of Romeo and Juliet in English class. I had to tweak part of the story and I was distracted, I couldn't focus. I drew this picture before I fell asleep, then when I woke up I was in Juliet's room, in your time."

"What do you mean, the 'play Romeo and Juliet'?" Paris asked, intrigued. "What is that?"

Harriet blew a breath out, searching for the best words to explain. "Well," she said. "It's like a story I suppose, except it's written in such a way that it tells different actors how to play the characters and what to say. This particular one was written about Romeo and Juliet." Harriet motioned to the pair of them. "They're quite the love story in modern times. Although it's strange," she said, frowning. "I don't really know why you guys are a love story. You're a pretty poor example of happily ever after."

"Why is that?" Paris asked. "How does this play end?"

"It's a tragedy," Harriet replied. "Juliet marries Romeo in secret. In the end, Juliet drinks the potion that I gave you, to make her appear dead so she can be released from her betrothal to you. But Romeo is banished to Mantua and he doesn't get the message from Friar Lawrence to tell him that Juliet is merely sleeping. He rushes to her side, killing you in the process for getting in his way. Romeo sees Juliet lying in the Capulet tomb and rushes to her side. He cries a bit, talks about how it's not fair. Then he drinks poison that he procured from Friar Lawrence." Harriet frowned. "Then as Romeo dies, Juliet wakes and shakes off the effects of her potion. But Romeo is lying beside her, dead, and so she wails at cruel fate and the unfairness of life. Then she takes Romeo's dagger and stabs herself to death."

Paris was staring at Harriet, open mouthed. "That sounds…terrible," he said. His gaze turned thoughtful. "So, if Romeo kills me then I suppose, in a way, you really saved the lives of all three of us by giving me that potion."

"That's what I was intending to do when I made that choice," Harriet replied. "I have to tell you; I was afraid it wouldn't end that way."

Paris turned his head to regard Caterina. "Was Lady Caterina in the…play?"

"No, she wasn't." Harriet rushed in before Caterina could say anything. "But she was a welcome addition after I drugged you. I would never have found Romeo and Juliet without her." Harriet smiled warmly at her friend.

Caterina took a deep breath and stepped forward. "Paris…my Lord," she said, her head bent humbly. "You honour me by calling me a Lady, however I am merely a servant in fair Verona. I have no honourable blood and no connections to call my own." Juliet frowned – that definitely wasn't the whole story.

"That's not entirely true though, is it Caterina?" Harriet said. In for a penny, in for a pound. She might as well call all in now, because their fate still rested on Paris' decision, to a large extent.

"Tell the entire story, Cat," Harriet urged quietly. Paris watched Caterina, his expression open and inviting her confidence. He patently wanted to hear what she had to say, and if Harriet's intuition was correct, it was unlikely to matter greatly to Paris if Caterina actually was a lowly servant. It might make life harder and throw a few more obstacles in their path, but what Harriet saw in Paris' face were the emotions that lay just beyond understanding and reasoning. It was the same look she saw on her father's face when he looked at her mother, or on her little brother's face when he saw a chocolate sundae. True, blind, crazy, total love.

Caterina twisted her fingers together. She steeled her nerves, then launched herself off the metaphorical cliff. It seemed she had decided to go all in too.

"My mother was the daughter of an English lord," Caterina began, trepidation evident in her voice. "She came to Verona on a trading mission with her father and never returned. She fell in love with my father, a simple stable hand. A daughter of the English nobility in love with a simple Italian man." Caterina's lips twisted in a self-deprecating smile as she told Paris her parents' love story.

"She died when I was five." Caterina finished sadly. "Since then I have been raised by my father and my brother. Unfortunately, my brother has been…persuaded by the local blacksmith to give him what he wants if my brother is to keep his business. Paolo Castile wants to marry me, and I will not consent." Caterina raised her chin a little in defiance.

"So…it seems to me that you are indeed Lady Caterina," Paris said, smiling at his beautiful blonde companion.

"I am not recognised in Verona as nobility," Caterina protested. "In fact, I don't believe I would be recognised in England either."

"You might be surprised," Paris said. "You're still entitled to apply for your birthright to be recognised in England. Is your grandfather still alive?"

Caterina shook her head. "I have no idea," she replied. "I've never met him, and I haven't heard anything about him since my mother died. She used to talk about him when I was little…I think she missed her home. She never regretted staying with my father…she loved him deeply. But I think she missed her family."

Paris didn't push further about her kinfolk or her status.

"So as I see it," Paris said. "I'm needed to speak with Escalus. I must tell him I've broken my betrothal to Juliet and convince him that Romeo is innocent of killing Tybalt. How am I to do this? I am supposed to be dead. Wouldn't I be due to be buried today?"

Romeo and Juliet both nodded. Paris looked contemplative. "So how am I meant to reappear from the dead?" he mused. "I could say that I took the wrong potion?"

Harriet chimed in, "What if you said that you had procured a potion to deal with your nerves about the wedding, but you accidentally received the wrong potion?"

"Yes!" Caterina added excitedly. "Then you could say that the fact you were so nervous told you that what you were about to do wasn't right for you, and that you want to call off your betrothal to Juliet."

"Excellent!" Juliet exclaimed. "You could also tell Escalus that you've spoken with me and we've agreed to release each other from our betrothal, because we both belong with other people."

"That could work," Paris said slowly. "Escalus will not be insulted by a lack of connection between us," he said to Juliet. "The wedding was pushed for by me, because I believed that I was in love with you. I hope you don't take offence, Lady Juliet, but I am certain that I am not in love with you. I am fond of you, but I absolutely do not feel the way that Romeo clearly does." Juliet turned to Romeo, her face glowing. Their salvation was closer, they were so near to being together, openly and safe from recriminations.

"But…," Paris said. "Where does everyone think you are, Juliet? Surely someone will have missed you by now. You've been gone for…how long?"

Harriet glanced at the sun. "Near on 24 hours now," she replied. She was getting good at telling the time without a watch. "Caterina and I took the road to Mantua just before lunch time yesterday. It's just a little earlier than that time now?" A nod of Romeo's head confirmed her assessment.

"There will have to be people looking for you, Juliet," Paris said. "How will we deal with that?"

"I think perhaps…," Romeo mused. "We need to find Escalus first and get his support, while avoiding anyone Capulet might have out searching for Juliet. Everything else comes from those two things being a success."

Paris nodded in agreement. "Then we best make our way to the Escalus tombs, without delay." He pivoted and held out his arm to

Caterina, who took it shyly. Romeo escorted both Harriet and Juliet across the expanse of the clear, grassy riverbank, trailing behind the magnificent pair in front, glowing in the sunshine.

Chapter Twelve

As they slipped back into the cobbled streets of Verona, they fell into single file and expanded the gap between the two little groups. Juliet pulled the hood of her cloak over her head – the last thing they needed was for people to see two women who looked near to identical running around the swankier part of town. Harriet also averted her face as they hurried through the laneways, trying not to attract any attention.

Both groups stopped in their tracks as they heard a sudden and urgent clatter of hooves on the cobblestones, thundering towards the lane they were in. A shout sounded as merchants were shoved out of the way by the incoming cavalcade of men mounted on horses.

Harriet saw a flash of brown fabric as Paris and Caterina disappeared into a gap between two buildings further up the street. Romeo pushed Juliet and Harriet into a similar space and squeezed in behind them. Harriet winced as a familiar, booming voice filled the air.

"Attention!" It was Capulet. And he was livid. "My daughter, Juliet, is missing. She has been absent from my home since yesterday and I demand any and all information that might lead to her discovery. Most of you will be aware of how Juliet looks…brown hair, brown eyes – she should be wearing a red and gold gown." Juliet glanced down at her dress, moaning as she realised it matched Capulet's description. He had clearly been searching through her wardrobe. She looked helplessly at Romeo. He grimaced.

"All information will be rewarded," Capulet continued to boom. "Those seeking the reward need to present what they know to me personally, at Capulet Castle. Spread the word." With that, Capulet yanked on his reins and turned awkwardly in the narrow street. His guard were already moving back down the street, scattering those out for a walk and running errands. Romeo stuck his head out of the gap and looked down the street to where Capulet had been. He saw Paris doing the same thing. They had been much closer to where Capulet had stopped.

It seemed that their plan now had some flaws in it. There was no way that either Juliet or

Harriet could swan around the streets of Verona – and Juliet was still dressed in the gown her father had advertised!

Harriet noticed that the narrow gap they were in opened up at the other end, and she followed the laneway twenty paces to the other end, peering curiously around the corner. She was looking at a small courtyard in between four tall, terracotta stained buildings. Between the walls of each was strung line after line, and on those lines were pinned billowing sheets and clothes. The dresses were simple but clearly belonged to someone who respected and loved them. They had been darned, scrubbed and hung out to dry in the bright sunlight. Harriet turned and motioned to the others to follow her before she ventured further into the courtyard.

Romeo gestured for Paris and Caterina to join them, then followed Juliet down the laneway. Before long, all five were standing in the little space, staring up at the drying linen.

"We have a problem," Paris stated. Juliet grimaced. She gestured down at her dress.

"I'm the poster child for a ransom reward," Juliet wailed, spreading her lovely skirt out to the sides. The red fabric shone in the sun and the gold glinted throughout, drawing the eye. It was very similar to the dress Harriet had worn for the engagement ball, but far less dazzling and intricate. Despite their activities of the last day, Juliet still looked wealthy. Her head dress was gone and her hair was loose, but there was something in her bearing that suggested she was of noble birth, even without the trappings. They couldn't do a great deal to stamp that out of her, but they could change her clothes. It seemed such a shame to take someone else's belongings, especially when they were so well cared for and clearly cherished.

Harriet eyed off a simple linen dress on the line. It was a forest green colour and would do nicely. She reached up and released it from its bindings, catching it before it dropped to the ground. Wordlessly, Harriet held the dress out to Juliet.

Juliet stared at it, then looked around at the small space and the number of people in it. "And how am I meant to change here?" Juliet demanded. Harriet rolled her eyes. Girls could be such princesses sometimes! Harriet carefully unfastened a sheet from the bottom line and gestured for Caterina to take one end. Caterina hurried over to grip the edge of the sheet and Harriet walked backwards, spreading the screening sheet wide.

"Ohhhh," said Juliet as Harriet's makeshift screen hid her completely from view. She quickly undid her own laces, proving far more adept at dressing herself than Harriet had been. Juliet snatched the green gown up and tossed it over her head, changing her garments as quickly as she possibly could.

Before long, Juliet stood dressed as a simple townswoman instead of a privileged young lady from a noble family. Harriet had slung the sheet back over the line and fastened it, and Caterina tidied any evidence that they had been there.

Juliet held up her red and gold dress and said, "What do I do with this?"

Caterina gestured for Juliet to hand her the dress. She rolled it tightly into a ball and placed it gently behind a stone wall jutting out into the little courtyard area. It wasn't visible to passers-by where it was, but it was easy enough for someone missing their own dress to find.

"Okay," Caterina said brightly. "Do we continue with the plan? Are we making our way to the Escalus tomb?"

"We have to pray that Escalus is still there," Paris said. "It's been some time now, and although Escalus is a patient man, he will only wait so long before he declares something is very wrong. As far as he knows, I'm dead and my body is now missing. That's enough to send anyone a little crazy. We have to try and get to him as quickly as possible, but we also don't want to spook his guards." The rest nodded their understanding.

The group split as they had before, into two smaller units. They made their way through the streets of Verona, wending their way to the tomb. Although it wasn't far to go, they had to stick to a pathway with plenty of spaces they could duck into at a moment's notice, and they had to make sure they always had an escape route. Harriet had no idea where they were going or how to get there, so she put her faith in the others and followed blindly. At times Romeo led, at others it was Caterina. As they got closer to the tomb Paris took over, and they slipped closer and closer to their goal, like spirits through a silent graveyard. They hadn't been spotted yet, or at least no one had yelled out or drawn attention to them.

Paris held up one hand and halted as he reached the corner of the laneway that led down to the crypts of Verona's oldest and most powerful families. The others stopped in their tracks behind him, trying their best to melt into their surroundings and appear inconspicuous. There weren't many people in this section of town, but there was no saying how long it would remain that way.

And in fact, they had their answer almost immediately. The sound of horses being ridden hard and fast broke the calmness and tranquillity of the quiet street. The five looked around in panic, looking for somewhere to hide. Harriet pointed to a low bush set back from the roadway and they all darted towards it. Romeo was the last one to take cover, and he dove behind the shrub just in time.

The horses came from both directions, filling the street with the sounds of hooves clopping, halters jingling and horses snorting. Harriet peeked through the leaves of their hiding place and saw Capulet and Escalus face to face, their horses nose to nose. Capulet looked furious and Escalus was well on his way to being in the same state.

"Escalus!" Capulet boomed. "My daughter is missing. There's no sign of her – I've got no idea where she is."

"I don't know what you're insinuating, Lord Capulet," Escalus said, his voice as cold as a winter's night in Siberia. "I know nothing about the whereabouts of your daughter. The body of my kinsman Paris is also missing. Do you have any information as to his whereabouts?" Escalus' voice dripped with disdain. "The Friar tells me that you arranged for his body to be moved to our vault. It is quite clear, however, this is not what has happened."

Capulet's face began dangerously red. He looked apoplectic with rage. "Are you accusing me of something, Escalus?" he bellowed, beyond caution and reason. Escalus met Capulet's spewing fire with icy rage.

"Tread carefully, Capulet." Escalus' voice was dangerously soft. Capulet didn't take the hint. He continued to rant about Paris and Juliet, rebellious teenagers and stress being the death of him. He muttered about the delay in the two being wed and railed against the unfairness of it all. Escalus merely watched with contempt as Capulet wound down.

"If you're quite finished, Lord Capulet," Escalus said frostily. "I'm busy looking for the body of my cousin. If you have no useful information to offer, kindly get out of my way." His tone invited no arguments and command rang in his tone and in every line of his face. Even Capulet, who had now calmed, couldn't fail to notice the coldly contained anger in the man in front of him. He eyed Escalus with resentment, but moved reluctantly to the side as Escalus steered his way through Capulet's men. They fell aside as the rest of Escalus' company moved through, heading back towards Verona from the family crypts.

The group hiding in the shrubbery looked at each other in despair. They had been too late, and they were now well and truly out of the frying pan and into the fire. Not only would the city be on alert for sightings of Juliet, Romeo was still banished and authorised to be killed on sight. On top of that, Escalus was using every ounce of his power to scour the city for Paris' body. Their glimpse of Capulet had shown a man on the rampage; a powerful Lord taking no prisoners. There was no telling what he would do if he caught sight of Romeo. Given what she'd seen of Capulet so far, Harriet was afraid he'd shoot first and ask questions later. Not that he could shoot…they had no guns in this time. But Harriet didn't think he'd hesitate to run Romeo through with a sword, or order one of his minions to do it for him.

Escalus and his cohort had ridden away, leaving Capulet and his men in their dust. The group watched from their hiding place as Capulet wheeled his horse around and addressed his men.

"It is time," Capulet's voice rang out, a militant glint in his eye. "We have dallied long enough. It is likely that Juliet has left the city. Courtesy of the kind blacksmith, we know that Romeo went to Mantua after his banishment, and we are aware that Juliet knows that too."

"Paolo!" Caterina whispered, her tone making the name sound like a swear word.

"We will ride for Mantua after lunch. Prepare the supplies, we will camp on the road overnight." Capulet's eyes swept over his assembled men. "Donato!" he barked, and a wiry, powerfully set gentleman moved forward out of the ranks, holding his horse's dancing head tightly.

"My Lord?" Donato asked, his head bent and deference clear in his tone.

"Donato…we will need to deal with that blasted Montague when we get to Mantua. I am leaving this in your hands. I expect him to be removed – permanently. Understood?" Donato nodded, his flat eyes unfeeling.

Juliet's sharp intake of breath was clearly audible among the little group on the other side of the greenery. Caterina put a hand on her friend's shoulder, trying to provide comfort. Romeo's face was grim and set, but also determined. Paris looked pensive. Harriet sat back on her heels and surveyed their little band. The sounds of Capulet and his men moving off into Verona filtered back to them in the same way the dappled sunlight leaked through to light the ground around them. It wouldn't be long before they'd have to start moving again, whether there was danger or not.

It was fortuitous that Capulet had decided to go to Mantua looking for Juliet. It was unlikely that he wouldn't travel with his men personally. After all, if there was a chance to see Romeo pay for the strife he'd visited on the house of Capulet, he would want to be there to see it. He was a vindictive sort of man and it was highly improbable he would miss an opportunity to see his foe pay for his actions. Juliet sat down heavily on the grass, sighing and covering her face with her hands. "What now?" she asked in a muffled voice.

Chapter Thirteen

"We have to get to Escalus," Paris said, his voice low and gravelly. He stood up and stretched full length before leaning against a nearby tree trunk. "If I know my cousin, he won't go home until my body is found. His pride won't allow him to." Paris frowned. "He'll set up a headquarters of sorts either at the Delser or at the Due Torri." Romeo grimaced. Juliet sighed.

Harriet looked confused. "So…what does that mean?" she asked. The names were all unfamiliar to her and she still had little clue as to where they were in Verona itself.

"It's either wonderful news, or terrible news," Juliet said with a sigh. She straightened from her spot behind the shrubs and brushed her dress off. "Due Torri is right next to the Sant'Anastasia church." Harriet's eyes lit up. "Don't get too excited," Juliet said wryly. "There's only a chance he'll go there. Delser is outside the city, in the same direction my father will go to get to Mantua." Harriet's face dropped.

Paris sighed. "It's also the same direction as Escalus' own estate. There's really no telling which way he'll go. He could go somewhere else entirely, but I don't think so. Escalus is a creature of habit."

"We're going to have to choose one and hope for the best," Romeo said, standing and brushing off his pants. "I vote that we choose the option that's less likely end with my head on a spike." Romeo and Paris looked at each other. "Due Torri," they said together.

Caterina stood and brushed her dress off. Despite everything they'd been through, she still looked as fresh as a daisy. Her long blonde hair still flowed down her back in a silky waterfall. Harriet's hair tried to follow suit, but it looked more like a mangled bird's nest.

Harriet pondered Caterina. Even though she was a remarkably pretty woman, Caterina didn't seem to notice or pay much attention to the way that she looked. She'd bounced out of the narrow, hard bed that morning looking like she'd rested for a solid twelve hours, despite her fractured and short sleep.

But while Caterina didn't notice her looks, it appeared that Paris certainly did. Harriet smiled a little to herself as she watched Paris, watching Cat. This was an interesting twist, she mused. Perhaps with a little bit of encouragement, a little push for Caterina to accept her rightful place in society, they could turn a tragedy into a double romance. After all, what else was she there for? There had to be some reason she'd fallen backwards in time half a millennium, and she didn't think that it was to make sure Romeo drank his poison and Juliet stabbed herself again.

"Due Torri is a wiser course," Caterina said, pacing lightly between the shrubbery and Paris' tree trunk. "The catacombs beneath the church will keep us mostly hidden, and we left a marker in the tunnel to show us which way to go."

"And if we make the wrong choice?" Juliet said, trepidation in her voice.

"Well, we're no worse off than we are standing here in the open," Caterina responded with forced cheerfulness. "Let's make our way back; we don't want to be on the streets of Verona when Capulet is ready to travel."

They all nodded their consent and checked their surroundings carefully before slipping back into the shadows. There were still remarkably few people around this part of town, and it puzzled Harriet. She slipped up next to Caterina.

"Why is it so quiet on the streets?" she asked the blonde phantom slipping silently through the shortening shadows. As the sun had risen to its highest point in the sky, there was limited cover available to them. They couldn't get back to the catacombs soon enough.

"Because no one comes out to do their business until after lunch," Caterina whispered back. "Mornings are for washing, cleaning and other domestic chores for the women and school and learning for the young men. The markets come alive at dusk, in the late afternoon when the weather cools down. It's too hot to bring out a lot of the goods for sale before that. Only a few vendors bother."

Harriet considered that. It made sense.

"That means we aren't going back for Juliet's dress just now?" Harriet asked. Caterina shook her head.

"Too risky," she replied. Harriet could see that Paris and Romeo, who were leading their little band, had chosen a different course back to the catacombs. She could only assume it was a shorter route and followed along instinctively. As they walked, Harriet mused that the trip back to somewhere always seems to be shorter than the travel there. Sure enough, before long the river came into sight and so did the bridge, with the grate to the catacombs just visible from where they stood. This was the riskiest part – it had the most open ground that they would need to cross. Their little group gathered together, measuring the distance.

While Caterina's face had already gone a pasty white – she remembered their first trip through the dark, musty tunnels – her chin was firm and she was determined not to let her fear show.

Paris took Caterina's elbow firmly, signalling his intention to accompany her across the riverbank. Romeo gripped Juliet's hand – a natural move that showed they often spent their time that way. Harriet sighed.

"I've never felt more like a fifth wheel," she joked lightly. "Do I go on my own, or am I crashing someone's party?"

Juliet laughed and linked arms with Harriet. She slung the dark green hood over her head and her face receded into the shadows.

"I have solved the problem," Juliet said brightly.

The group of three went first – they were the most conspicuous. Paris and Caterina followed behind. They would have looked like a pair of lovers out for a stroll along the riverbank, except for the stark difference in their attire. Paris was dressed as befitted the close relation of a prince, albeit slightly dusty and dirty. Caterina's servant's gown should have made her look lowly and unkempt, but somehow she still looked radiant and beautiful. The happiness and wonder of new love was blooming on her face, and her feelings were mirrored in the way Paris looked down at her as she spoke, or smiled as she said something amusing. Harriet snuck a quick glance back at them and smiled quietly at what she saw. Love was definitely blossoming for those two. There was undeniable potential here to change more than one storyline.

The first group reached the catacomb entrance and waited, shrouded in the shadows and damp for the second pair. Before long, they were ready to travel back through the darkness to the altar of the Sant'Anastasia. The natural light only reached as far as the first turn in the tunnel and they knew that beyond lay inky darkness.

Harriet wasn't afraid of small spaces or darkness. She had spent many an enjoyable hour with her brothers playing spotlight and hide and seek, squished into the tiniest and darkest of hiding spots. She knew that they would emerge into the light at the other end, but she equally knew that Caterina would struggle. It didn't look like she needed to worry though, and she smiled slightly as Paris slid his hand down Caterina's arm and took her hand, leading the way into the black. Romeo and Juliet had already headed in and Harriet swung into line in between the two couples.

The only sounds as they made their way back through the pitch darkness was the shuffle of their feet on stone and Caterina's breathing, which she was trying hard to control. It didn't seem as laboured as the first trip though, and Harriet wondered if it was Paris' presence and support that made the difference, or if she had grown a little more accustomed to her surroundings. Either way, the improvement was very welcome.

They quickly arrived at the round room, the multitude of tunnels spanning off the circle, dark and ominous. It would have been as unsettling as the first time they stumbled upon the confusing labyrinth, except Juliet's bright gold scarf hung limply from the crevice it had been tucked into several hours before. It showed there really was little fresh air in the tunnels, and it would be prudent for them to move on as quickly as possible.

Romeo looked longingly at the other tunnels.

"I'd love to see where they go," he said wistfully.

"I'd love to not see your head on a spike, dearest," Juliet replied sweetly, taking his hand and tugging him through the tunnel they needed. She grabbed her scarf on the way through, bunching it up in her hand.

All too soon they were back in the small hallway of the rectory, but there was no one in sight. They could hear the murmur of voices, music and what sounded like chanting. Juliet held her hand up and they all halted where they were and listened.

"It's a mass," Juliet said quietly, as she moved closer to the door they knew led to the altar of the church.

"It must be the midday mass," Caterina said in a strained whisper. "That can go for over an hour!"

"No, listen," Paris said, his finger to his lips. Harriet was thoroughly confused. Her family weren't churchgoers and she had little idea what a mass even was. She assumed it was a mass of people perhaps, so a gathering, but as for what happened during it, she was clueless.

"See, hear the shuffle of feet," Paris said, moving closer to the door and taking Caterina with him. They all listened.

"They're moving away from the altar. They're breaking the bread and drinking the wine,"

Paris said, a frown on his face as he listened intently. "There can't be long to go now."

"We'll have to wait," Juliet sighed. "We can't go outside the church, there will be people leaving and we can't be seen."

"We need to speak to Friar Lawrence anyway," Harriet said. The others looked at her in surprise. "This story is already vastly different to the version I know of Romeo and Juliet," Harriet said wryly. "I have no clue what's meant to happen next: we're making a new story now."

"Well, we have some time to wait," Paris said, settling himself down on the stony ground and leaning against the wall. Caterina sat gracefully beside him. To anyone who took the time to look, she was clearly a great deal more than a merchant's sister.

"Why don't you tell us the story of Romeo and Juliet, as you know it," Paris said. Harriet considered. Why not? They had time to kill.

"Okay," she said, sitting cross legged in the hallway. The long skirts of the dress she wasn't used to spread out around her like a puddle. Romeo and Juliet made themselves comfortable too.

"Keep in mind, I did skip through some sections of the story," Harriet said, frowning. "I've told you some parts. At the beginning it talks about bad blood between two families in Verona, the Montagues and the Capulets." Romeo and Juliet nodded.

Harriet continued. "The Capulets have a party and the Montagues and their friends decide to attend the party without an invitation. This is where Romeo meets Juliet. Romeo then sneaks up to Juliet's window after the party and calls out to her. She comes out and they declare their love for each other." The others were nodding. "Romeo and Juliet see Friar Lawrence and are married in secret, with no witnesses other than the Friar himself."

"Well that part's wrong," Caterina interjected. "I was there!" Then she remembered herself and looked apologetically at Paris. He waved her concern away.

"So then after the marriage, Romeo was called to a fight between the Montagues and Capulets, a big one. Romeo's friend, Mercutio, was killed by Tybalt, a Capulet, and Romeo chased him to seek revenge."

Romeo was shaking his head vehemently. So was Paris.

"That's not what happened," they both said together. Romeo nodded at Paris, indicating that he should go first.

"I went to see Capulet, to ask for Juliet's hand in marriage," Paris said. "Until then I had no idea there was a link between Juliet and Romeo, much less that they were already married. That part is true, you were married?" Paris peered at the couple through the gloom. They nodded.

Paris continued. "Capulet told me that there was a Montague standing in the way of a union between myself and Juliet, but that he would be removed and it would not be an impediment to our marriage. We were in Capulet's study and he asked me to wait for a moment while he sent a message. His footman came in and took it not two minutes later, so it cannot have been a lengthy message." Paris frowned. "I was making small talk with Capulet and he was keen to establish a betrothal between Juliet and I as a matter of urgency. He asked me to call back later in the afternoon."

Juliet interjected. "That would have been the afternoon that Father visited me in my room and told me I was to be married to you. I told him I would not." She looked at Paris apologetically. "It's nothing personal, you understand. My heart is with Romeo, and besides, I was already married just that morning. Polygamy is a sin in the eyes of the church and punishable by law. I was in quite a situation." Paris nodded. His demeanour suggested that he was not personally affected by Juliet's words. Harriet observed, heartened by the apparent shift in loyalties and attention on Paris' behalf.

"So my father struck me. He demanded that I would attend my engagement ball the next evening or I would be thrown out of the house. My mother wailed for hours, but ultimately she's ineffective where Father is concerned. She loves me, I know, but she simply can't or won't stand up to him. She advised me to follow Father's orders and left me, or so she thought, picking out a dress for the wedding that was to follow within the week. The banns were to be read at the next church service and our betrothal celebrated at a ball at Capulet Manor."

"I was asked to stay until the ball," Paris continued, picking up where Juliet had left off. "In preparation, I sent footmen to collect clothes from the Escalus estate and to send the happy tidings to my cousin."

"I was also in residence at Capulet Manor that evening," Romeo stated sheepishly. Juliet coloured.

"Yes well, the less said about THAT, the better," Caterina said hurriedly. "What happened next?"

"Well," Juliet said pensively. "When I woke the next morning, Nurse brought me news that Romeo had been banished from Verona. Obviously, I was very surprised and naturally upset. I wanted to know why, and all she could tell me was that Tybalt had been cut down in cold blood, by Romeo, and that Mercutio was dead."

"I heard the same news," Paris concurred. "The news was brought to me that Mercutio, my cousin, had been killed by Tybalt and before Escalus could find Romeo to bring an end to the violence, he stumbled across Tybalt's body with Romeo's blade still embedded in his stomach." Paris looked apologetically at the ladies. "My apologies, this is not exactly proper and appropriate conversation for our company."

"Nonsense," Caterina said dismissively. "How else will we get to the truth of this mess?" Harriet nodded approvingly. The girl had found her voice, and an intelligent one it was. Caterina was not a woman to be trifled with and she commanded respect, as a merchant's daughter or an Italian/English noblewoman.

"Harriet, tell us the story that you know." Juliet asked, a frown between her eyes.

"Well," Harriet said. "The brawl between the Capulets and Montagues occurred around the middle of the day. Mercutio taunted Tybalt and was killed in the fight between the two sides. Romeo, overcome with hatred, chased Tybalt and put a blade through him. It began over a suspected relationship between Romeo and Juliet. Tybalt was said to be enraged that his cousin was considering an alliance with a Montague and he wanted his head."

"Well, that much is true," Juliet said wryly. "Tybalt would rather have died than have seen Romeo and I together, such was his hatred for the Montague house. Odd, considering nothing has ever really happened in our lifetime to generate such ill feeling. But the bad blood goes back a long way and Tybalt was under the tutelage of my father his whole life. My father certainly has an unfathomable hatred for the Montagues and he passed that onto Tybalt."

"So what's the missing link here?" Paris said, frowning. "Something isn't adding up. Clearly you didn't tell Tybalt you had married Romeo in secret," Paris said, turning to Juliet. She shook her head. "Did anyone but Caterina know you had married?"

"Nurse did," Juliet said. "That is why she brought the news to me so quickly. She was disapproving of our marriage but ultimately she helped us. She was a go between with Friar Lawrence, Romeo and I."

"So only two other people knew of the marriage," Paris said slowly. "And I doubt you'd be keen to go knocking on your new father in law's door with the news," Paris said with a nod to Romeo. Romeo shook his head wryly.

"So how did Tybalt find out, and in enough time to arrange a good contingent of Capulets to fight. But wait…maybe we're getting this all wrong. I didn't hear of a disturbance in Verona that day. I was a little distracted, but I surely would have heard about an all and out brawl. What exactly did Nurse say to you, Juliet?"

Romeo answered. "She said that I had killed Tybalt in cold blood and had been banished to Mantua. She mentioned Mercutio's death as an afterthought, something that didn't really seem connected to the first news." The others stared at Romeo. "I was under the bed," he said, a chagrined look on his face. "It was very early in the morning!"

"Nurse didn't want to waste time telling me," Juliet explained. "We smuggled Romeo out, because Nurse had been told if his face was seen in Verona he would be killed on sight. It was still pre-dawn, so we both set off for

Mantua. We stopped to rest at the hut Caterina had told Nurse about. I was not letting Romeo go without me, we would face what was coming together and I didn't care what my father had to say about it. Escaping Verona was easy. We took Star, but we had only one horse between us. We stopped at the hut and stayed there in case anyone decided to pursue Romeo to Mantua, much as my dear Father suggested earlier." There was a bitterness in Juliet's voice. She knew her father was ruthless and could be cold, but hearing him order Romeo's death had shaken her deeply.

"So," Harriet said slowly. "You left before dawn…I awoke in your room on the day of the ball celebrating your betrothal to Paris. You left as I arrived!"

"Yes, and how did you arrive, exactly?" Paris asked. "The two of you could be mistaken for the same person. I didn't notice any differences the night of the ball, except that your dancing was a little rustier than I had expected. I suppose that makes sense now." Harriet stuck her tongue out at Paris good naturedly. He looked puzzled and clearly didn't know how to respond. Harriet started speaking quickly to fill the awkward silence.

"All I know is that I drew a picture that night before I went to sleep. The drawing melded my face with Juliet's and it ended up my hand while I was asleep. I remember thinking it was stormy and windy that night, but I might have been dreaming. I don't know. When I awoke I was here, in Verona, about to be clothed for a betrothal ball and trying to figure out where on earth I was. I believe the drawing is the key and I'm keeping it safe, with me. I'm not letting it out of my reach."

"Could we see it again?" Caterina asked, intrigued.

Harriet reached inside the sleeve of her dress and unsnagged the paper from where she'd securely tucked it. She unfolded it from the small square it had become. As she did, a lead drawing of a beautiful face emerged. It had the beauty and grace of Juliet's face, combined with the strength, determination and wilfulness of Harriet's face.

The two could be mistaken for the same woman from afar, or by people who didn't know them, but if one knew the temperament of each they were unmistakably different. They had been raised in different times, by different parents and with different ideals. It was hardly a surprise that there would be disparities between the two – after all, they were individuals – but during the time they'd known each other, they'd both come to resemble the drawing more closely. Juliet's eyes showed a determined glint – she was not going to let anything get in the way of her happiness with Romeo. And a softer patience was evident in Harriet's face. She had matured, and her time in Verona had shown her that rushing headlong into everything didn't always yield the best outcome. Sometimes a canny and measured silence served just as well as a scream or shout.

Caterina eyed the drawing, then looked as the faces of each of the other two women. "Huh," she said. Caterina could see the incremental changes as well. Both of the men saw a pretty drawing but weren't as attuned to the changes in the ladies.

"Okay, so that's probably the key to getting you back home," Caterina said. "Where is home?"

Harriet's eyes went dreamy. "Wineglass Bay, in Tasmania," she said. Then frowned. "That's right, Europe hasn't discovered Australia yet. It's beautiful. We have the loveliest beaches and oceans. In the summer it's warm and breezy and in the winter it snows sometimes, especially during big storms and really cold years. The air is so clear and fresh. I hear that it's much like Scotland, but I wouldn't know. I haven't ever been there. I have a family there," Harriet's expression turned wistful. Caterina's turned sympathetic. "My parents and two brothers. The boys can be annoying, sure, but I'm certainly missing them now. I think I might take them for granted a little bit." Harriet thoughts turned inward, to cherished memories of her family. The rest of the group mulled over the puzzle of Romeo's banishment and Mercutio's death; specifically, how it linked to Tybalt's murder.

"So here's what I'm thinking," Paris said. Harriet came back to the present as he spoke. "Romeo could not have killed Tybalt. He was with Juliet when the body was found, in the late afternoon from what we've all heard. Mercutio's demise we don't know that much about, but we do know it isn't likely there was a large affray, as in the story that Harriet knows. So, was there a fight between Mercutio and Tybalt? And why? Mercutio is a lover, not a fighter. He doesn't get involved in the politics between the two families, in just the same way that Escalus and I do not. We're charged with keeping the peace, and getting in the middle of a blood war between two families is not the way to do that."

Juliet sat up straighter from her position on the floor. "Paris," she said slowly. "You said that my father wrote a letter and gave it to his footman. When was that?" Paris frowned, trying to remember.

"It would have been just after lunch, perhaps around 2 o'clock? My footman was dispatched around half two to fetch Escalus and my clothes. Come to think of it, he reported no disturbance when he returned that evening and he surely would have. That means that if Escalus was involved in dealing with whatever happened, it had to have been after my footman left the estate." Paris frowned. "He couldn't have left before five o'clock, by the time he rode there, packed and returned. He was back at the Capulet Manor by 6 o'clock, just in time for the evening meal."

Juliet's frown darkened. She stood and paced the small area they were all crowded into. They had forgotten about the mass taking place in the room beside them – their whole attention was focussed on the conundrum before them. Caterina stood as well, and silently regarded her friend's agitated state.

"Do you think he's capable of it, Juliet?" Caterina asked quietly. Juliet continued to pace, her arms folded over her stomach.

"I don't want to think that he is," she replied. "But after today…how could you not?"

Paris' tone was patience personified. "Ladies…would you care to tell the rest of us what you're thinking?"

"Juliet thinks that her father has something to do with this," Romeo said.

"Do you two have the same mind or something?" Paris exclaimed.

"He's right," Juliet said, swinging around to face the group. "That's exactly what I'm thinking. What if that note was to Tybalt. Tybalt would do anything my father asked of him, without question. None of us know what the note said, but someone had to kill Mercutio to make it look like Romeo killed Tybalt in revenge."

"Then who killed Tybalt?" Paris said, confused.

"It wouldn't surprise me if Donato did it," Caterina said, shuddering. "That man gives me the creeps. His eyes are so cold."

"Donato is Father's henchman," Juliet confirmed. "He does the things that no one else has the stomach for. Of course, this is all speculation. How do we confirm any of it? Until we have a real answer, Romeo's safety is still in great peril and I'm not in a good way myself."

Paris answered. "We have to get to Escalus," he said, repeating his edict from earlier.

"There's also the small matter of him looking for my body."

The group was distracted by a ruckus from beyond the door to the altar.

"Lawrence!" boomed a now familiar voice. The service was clearly over. And Escalus had arrived. They had been hoping the Friar would return to his quarters so they could speak with him before Escalus, but it looked like this was happening now. The group looked at each other in panic.

"I can't just walk out there," Paris hissed. He had sprung to his feet and was gesturing to himself. "He'll think the devil's work is at play."

"I can't walk out there," Romeo said. "He could arrest me on sight, and we may not get another chance."

Juliet and Harriet looked at each other. "We aren't a great deal of use, we'd confuse the poor man more," Juliet said.

"In fact, Harriet," Paris said, frowning. "Perhaps Escalus shouldn't see you at all. He's a logical man, and anything he can't explain with logic he tends to see as the work of dark forces. He can be very black and white like that. Perhaps you could remain hidden until we come up with a better way to explain you?"

Harriet nodded.

"Guess that leaves me then," Caterina said brightly, adjusting her plain dress and smoothing her hair. "How do I look?" she joked.

"Perfect," Paris said, smiling at her. "Tell him slowly," he instructed. "And briefly. We can fill in the rest later. All he really needs to know right now is that I'm not dead." Caterina nodded. She took a deep breath and gripped the ring handle of the plain door into the church.

"Wish me luck," she whispered.

Chapter Fourteen

Caterina walked out of the darkness into blinding light and utter confusion. The church was filled with Escalus and his men, all advancing on the little old Friar standing at the ornate altar ablaze with candles. He had clearly been about to snuff out some of those candles as the party of armed men arrived, but had halted in his tracks when confronted with the cold anger of Escalus.

"Where is my cousin!" Escalus demanded, his tone icy. The Friar looked panicked – he had lost his usual calm in the unexpected intrusion so soon after his peaceful service had concluded.

Caterina emerged from the shadows beside the altar. A military man, Escalus' attention shifted instantly to the plain, pretty maiden who was moving quietly and unobtrusively to stand between Escalus and Friar Lawrence. The Friar had been Caterina's religious mentor her whole life – she was as invested in nothing bad befalling him as she was in protecting the others.

"Prince Escalus," she began, her hands spread wide and her courtesy low and deep. "My name is Caterina, and I am friend to Juliet Capulet. I have much to tell you. Please, won't you all take a seat?"

In the face of such politeness and refined speech from a young woman who was dressed as though she ought to be hanging out laundry or mending clothes, Escalus didn't know what to do. He looked around at his men and nodded, and there was a clatter as they all sat on the wooden church pews, their swords clanging on the ancient and smooth chairs.

"Please, Mistress Caterina, tell your story," Escalus said, with a great deal more chivalry than he had shown Friar Lawrence. Paris knew what he had been doing when he sent Caterina out to see Escalus, but he was still fervently praying, glued to the door dividing them, that she come to no harm. He trusted his cousin but still he stood, ready to intervene, if such a situation arose.

"You see, My Lord, it is quite the story," Caterina said with a touch of humour in her voice. "I know not all of it, but I know enough to tell you that things are very much not as they seem. For example, your cousin, Paris? I believe that you are looking for his body?"

Escalus growled and looked at the Friar. Caterina held out her hands soothingly, almost hypnotising Escalus into returning his attention to her.

"As I said before, I am a friend to Juliet Capulet. She was betrothed to marry Paris, right before an accident befell him. I am sorry to say that Juliet was the cause of the accident, but am very happy to tell you that Paris is well and alive."

Escalus sprang up from his seat. "You lie!" He shouted, forgetting himself in his grief and anger. "I saw his body, I grieved over his body. He lay here in preparation for burial and he had no breath, no colour. I saw him with my own eyes. And now you tell me my eyes are lying?" Escalus had advanced on Caterina in his rage and frustration without even realising he had done so. Friar Lawrence had moved closer, intent on protecting Caterina from Escalus' fury, no matter the cost to himself.

"The young lady speaks true," Friar Lawrence said with a sigh. "I provided the sleeping draught myself. There is another story behind that; it was not actually intended for your cousin. As to how he came to drink it…well, maybe the young lady has the answer to that too.”

“I do,” Caterina said, refusing to be cowed by Escalus. She had dealt with much angrier, less stable men before. She knew he was confused and in pain, two things she knew a great deal about. “But perhaps it might help if I could prove to you that Paris is alive, and then we can fill in the story from there?” Escalus eased his grip on his sword and stepped back from Caterina, nodding his consent.

Caterina walked quietly to the separating door and swung it open, revealing Paris awash in the light of the altar candles.

“By God,” Escalus breathed, rushing over to his cousin. Paris moved towards Escalus and they wrapped each other in a manly hug, patting each other on the back.

“I thought you were dead,” Escalus said, his voice unsteady.

“I know,” Paris said, his voice low and gravelly. “I was surprised to wake up in here also. But there is quite the story behind it, and perhaps you can help us with it?” Escalus nodded uncertainly. The two moved to sit back on the front pew. Escalus couldn’t take his eyes off Paris; it was like he had risen from the dead.

Caterina assumed that the others had chosen to remain hidden for now. Probably prudent, given Escalus' initial reaction to Paris being alive. She moved to stand unobtrusively to the side, between the pew and the open door.

"Cousin, there is something foul afoot," Paris said. "But first, I will start at the beginning. Capulet accepted my offer for Juliet's hand, as you know. We had our betrothal ball, but that was not as it seemed. Juliet was not my partner that night, but a distant…cousin…stood in her place. Juliet had fled to Mantua with Romeo, after they heard of the banishment and the bounty on his head." Escalus went to interject but Paris stopped him. "Let me finish first, I think it might be less confusing. So from there, Juliet – or rather, her cousin – came to my room that night, after the ball. We spoke and toasted our betrothal together, but my ale was drugged with sleeping potion. From what I understand, the plan was for Juliet to drink the potion to appear dead, so she would be released from her betrothal to me, however when Romeo – her newly wedded husband – was banished she went with him instead. I know nothing from then until after I awoke, but Caterina can fill us in on some of the rest." Paris held out his hand invitingly to Caterina. She picked up the story.

"Juliet – or so I thought – asked me to travel with her to Mantua, to seek out Romeo. I did not know that Juliet had actually gone very early the morning before, or that her…cousin…was acting in her place. I figured it out when we met up with Romeo and Juliet later that day, which was quite confronting. We raced back here to save Paris from being interred in the vault – once he was in there, we had no idea how to unseal it and get him back out."

"There would have been no way short of smashing through very thick rock," Escalus said wryly.

"Indeed," Paris said. "I owe my new friends a great debt of gratitude. And in fact…one of those friends includes Romeo Montague." Escalus tensed. "Hear me out, cousin," Paris continued earnestly. "Something is not right in this story. Before we continue, can you tell me about the deaths of Mercutio and Tybalt Capulet?"

Escalus sighed. "It was a very odd business indeed. Mercutio was found at dusk, a single dagger blade through his heart. It matched the dagger that Tybalt carries. We went searching for Tybalt, and for Romeo, given that we know how close he was to Mercutio. We were worried there would be an all-out war between the Capulets and Montagues over this one. We couldn't find Romeo; he had gone to ground somewhere." Caterina and Paris exchanged a knowing look. "But Tybalt we found. His body was in an alley near the main square, with a dagger emblazoned with Romeo's crest still sticking out of him. I issued the banishment for Romeo, but if he were to be seen in Verona he was to be brought to me."

Paris frowned. "Different to our version then," he murmured.

"And what exactly is your version?" Escalus asked.

"Romeo was told that he was banished to Mantua for killing Tybalt, which he cannot have done. I cannot explain why, that isn't my story to tell. But I believe that he cannot have done so." Friar Lawrence was nodding his head earnestly.

Paris continued. "Romeo and Juliet both fled to Mantua, because they had also been told there was a bounty on Romeo's head and he was to be killed on sight. They left in the dark hours of the morning to avoid such an event." Escalus frowned.

"Those were most definitely not my orders," he growled.

"There's more, cousin," Paris said. "When I was in Capulet's study speaking with him about my betrothal to Juliet, he sent a missive off to someone. I know not who, but it was a short letter and it didn't take him long to write. Juliet's Nurse also said that there was talk of a street brawl between the Montagues and Capulets, which is how Mercutio had died, and that Romeo had pursued Tybalt and killed him in revenge."

Escalus' frown deepened. "That is just patently untrue," he said. "There is no way an affray between those two families would pass unnoticed in this town. I would likely have been tied up for days with the consequences of such a brawl. But who would spread such an untruth, and why?"

"I think I may know," Caterina said quietly. "But mind, I have little proof. Earlier when we were trying to find you to explain all of this, we ran into Capulet and his men. We heard him order his men to prepare for a trip to Mantua, and for Donato to kill Romeo once they got there. We think that perhaps Capulet knows of the marriage between Romeo and Juliet and he wants revenge. He believes that Paris is dead, but he is not a man to be crossed."

"This Donato I have heard of," Escalus said, ponderingly. "He is a most unpleasant man, very cold and calculating." Then his voice rang out.

"Romeo. Juliet. Reveal yourselves." All three of the remaining fugitives came out slowly from behind the door and lined up in front of the altar. Escalus studied them one by one.

"Yes," he said. "I can see the difficulty in telling the difference between the two ladies. Who is the second young lady?"

"Lady Harriet, my Lord," Juliet said hastily. Escalus nodded as Juliet curtseyed. Harriet hastily copied her moves. His stare returned to Romeo.

"I am told that there is no way you could have killed Tybalt," Escalus said. "How is this so?" Romeo looked at Juliet, embarrassed. Juliet's chin firmed.

"My Prince, he could not have killed Tybalt because he was with me. That can be confirmed by both Friar Lawrence and Nurse. We were married in the morning and we spent the rest of the afternoon in Capulet Manor, out of my father's sight. Except for the short period where he came in and commanded I marry Paris, but Romeo was hidden during that exchange."

Escalus looked slightly taken aback to see the confident, mature young woman in front of him speaking about matters that were usually screened from ladies, but he took it in his stride remarkably well.

"So you were commanded to marry Paris, yet you were already married to Romeo, who was also hiding in the room listening to all of this?" Escalus confirmed. "That's quite the situation."

"Especially when Capulet struck and threatened Juliet," Romeo growled.

"There's nothing you could have done about it," Juliet said in a low aside. "Your head would already be on a spike." It was clearly an issue that bothered Romeo – it abraded his male sensibilities that he had been unable to protect his wife – but his wife had done an admirable job of protecting him.

One of Escalus' commanders stirred and beckoned to his master. Escalus rose and moved a short distance away, listening intently to his man's whispered words. His shoulders straightened.

"It would appear that we have more than one reason to question this Donato," Escalus said, but clearly not in a mood to explain further. "I will issue a proclamation removing your banishment, Romeo, but I would suggest that you lay low until word reaches every part of the town. And until I have Lord Capulet in my custody for questioning." He turned to Paris.

"And you, my cousin. You have not come out of all this too well. Poisoned, jilted…I do not envy you, my kin."

Paris smiled. "Sometimes the world works in mysterious ways, Cousin," he said. He captured Caterina's hand and brought it to his lips. "It would appear that there is a lady better suited to me, if she will have me." Caterina looked stunned. "But Paris, you can't…my reputation…"

"Who exactly is this young lady?" Escalus said, looking alarmed. "Paris, I can't condone reckless behaviour and ill-gotten marriages. We are role models in this town, and what we do, others will too." Caterina's eyes were on the floor.

"This young woman is Lady Caterina, and her grandfather is a member of the English nobility. He is a Marquise," Juliet answered, her eyes flashing. "She is no mere maiden. Her…circumstances…have forced her into accepting a life that is beneath her and she is due to be married to the most god awful man."

"Who?" Escalus asked.

"Paolo, the blacksmith," Caterina said quietly. Escalus made a sound of disgust mixed with pity.

"And are you English nobility?" Escalus asked Caterina.

"Well," Caterina began, looking nervously at the thirty or so soldiers hanging on her every word. Harriet looked at them too. Each man was solely focused on the words coming out of Caterina's mouth as she told her tale, from the powerful meeting of two lovers meant for each other, to Margaret's tragic death.

Escalus was also paying close attention to the lovely young woman in front of him and while he listened to her words, he also observed how his cousin regarded the lady. Paris was clearly smitten, and he could tell it would take a great deal of effort to divert him from this course.

Harriet's attention snapped to Paris as his voice broke into the conversation.

"Cousin, clearly you can see that this is an extraordinary situation. I intend to call on Caterina's father and offer for her hand in marriage. My apologies," he said, turning to Caterina. "I realise that is the wrong way around, but I do not want there to be any misunderstandings. I significantly outrank Paolo; I will replace any dowry that he demands in return for your cancelled betrothal."

Caterina simply stood there, stunned. Juliet was overjoyed and her pleasure at her friend's happiness was beaming from her face. Harriet cheered silently that Caterina would not have to face the detestable Paolo.

Escalus looked thoughtful. "I can tell from the young lady's bearing that she was not raised a barn maid. But all of this is for later! For now, there is work to be done. Men! We are seeking Capulet and Donato, as well as any other men in Capulet's employ who can shed light on the events of the last few days. They were preparing to head to Mantua to seek Romeo – how long ago?"

"Perhaps an hour?" Paris guessed, looking at the others for confirmation. They nodded.

"Excellent," Escalus said. "We should reach the town border before he does. To the Mantua road, with haste." Escalus turned back to their little ragged band. "I have set up headquarters in Due Torri," Escalus said to Paris. "You can enter my suite via the usual location. I suggest you use it and remain there until I return. Do not move." His gaze swept over them all, before he turned to Friar Lawrence.

"My apologies, Friar Lawrence," Escalus said sincerely.

The Friar waved them away. "You were grieving, my Lord."

"In any event." With one last look at the assembled group, Escalus led his men away from the altar and out through the grand front entrance of the church.

***

As Escalus and his men thundered through the streets of Verona in pursuit of Capulet and his entourage, the little band of friends snuck out of the Sant'Anastasia and into the side alleys beside the Due Torri.

The hotel was relatively unassuming, especially as an establishment chosen by a Prince. It sat in the Piazza, baking in the hot afternoon Italian sun. Its light brown walls shimmered as the heat bounced off them and most of the white and green shutters shading the hotel rooms were firmly closed against the sun.

The group paused in the short shadows between the Due Torri and the lighter building beside it. They watched as Paris measured the distance between the ground and a first floor balcony decorated with a delicate, wrought iron balustrade. Like a cat, Paris bounced on the balls of his feet before pushing upwards, jumping to catch the bottom ledge of the balcony.

"Heavens," Caterina whispered.

"It's not that impressive," Romeo said dismissively. "Juliet's balcony is much higher than this one." He grinned, showing there was no malice in his comment. Juliet made at face at her husband. Paris had swung himself up and over the iron railing and was standing, looking down at the remaining four.

"Romeo, if you boost the ladies up, I can grip their arms from here and pull them up over the railing. Just check the Piazza before we do, it wouldn't take much for someone to spot us." Relaxed in the company of his friends, Paris had reverted back to much less formal speech. They all had. Escalus had a way of bringing out the formality in everyone.

Romeo walked nimbly to the corner of the building and looked both ways, before returning to stand underneath the balcony.

"Still empty," he said with a shrug.

"Good," said Paris. "But let's get this over with, before we have any unwanted guests." He beckoned for Caterina to be passed up to him first.

Romeo grasped Caterina's waist and hoisted her up. Paris lifted her easily over the railing and set her on her feet. A slight blush stained Caterina's cheeks.

"Juliet next," Paris commanded. Romeo grinned and grabbed his bride around the waist, hoisting her up too. She was light as a feather in her borrowed dress, and she sailed up and over the balcony as well. The balcony was fast becoming crowded and there was little room for Paris to manoeuvre.

"Wait a moment," Paris called down softly to Harriet and Romeo. He turned and pushed open the long shutters screening the door into the suite. He motioned the two women through, before turning back to Romeo and Harriet still loitering in the shadows below.

Romeo hesitated to put his hands around Harriet's waist. Instead, he bent down as low as he could on one knee, deeming it a more gentlemanly approach. Harriet hiked the bottom of the dress she wasn't used to up to her calves and stepped on Romeo's bent knee, balancing with one hand on his head.

"Not quite as graceful," she said ruefully.

"As long as we get you up there in one piece," Romeo said. "Shoulders now."

Harriet's tongue stuck out between her teeth as she concentrated on placing her feet correctly on Romeo's shoulders. He held his hands up and Harriet grasped them for balance. Romeo was crouching, Harriet balanced on his shoulders, and he slowly rose to stand full length. Harriet's height combined with Romeo's meant that if it weren't for the balustrade, Harriet could simply have stepped onto the balcony. Paris grasped Harriet's hands and helped her to turn and sit on the railing, before tipping her backwards and assisting her to stand on the balcony.

"There," he said, smiling. "Still graceful in many ways. Get up here, Romeo."

Romeo bounced up onto the balcony in much the same way Paris had, with ease and agility. It seemed Italian men, or at least these ones, were adept at climbing.

Harriet joined Juliet and Caterina in the suite occupied by Escalus. There were arched doorways that led to different spaces within the one room and despite outward appearances, the inside of the Due Torri was opulent and well appointed. The furniture was immaculate and ornate and the ceilings were decorated with painted angels and frescos.

Harriet's eyes were huge as she took in her surroundings. They were certainly grander than anything she was used to in Australia. The hotels in the main streets of Launceston and Hobart perhaps, but they'd always stayed at fun family hotels when their family had gone on holidays. Perhaps one day, when she was older, she'd look for this kind of luxury when she went and stayed away from home. But for now it was slightly overwhelming, and a little overbearing. Juliet's room had seemed more comforting somehow, more welcoming and familiar. This was another level again.

"So," Paris said, waving the ladies to seats in what appeared to be a lavish sitting room. "What must we do from here? Escalus is on his way to find Capulet and he will be questioned, mark my words. Escalus is not a stupid man, and the fact that he knows of Donato does not bode well for Capulet's henchman. What else must we do in the meantime?"

"If you don't mind," Caterina said, her hands primly crossed in her lap. "I wouldn't mind having a private discussion with Juliet and Harriet." She looked uncomfortable voicing her request, but she persevered doggedly. "Much has changed since we met with Prince Escalus, and I would like a moment to absorb that somewhat." Caterina looked and sounded every inch of the English nobility she was born to be, albeit with an Italian accent.

Paris nodded and stood immediately. Romeo stood as well, though a little more reluctantly, and followed Paris from the room. He knew this was going to be quite the conversation.

As soon as they left, Juliet turned to Caterina and gripped her hands excitedly. "Cat," she said breathlessly. "You are to be married!"

"Settle," Caterina said, her eyes reflecting joy mixed with uneasiness. "My family is still another matter altogether."

"Cat!" Juliet exclaimed. "Do you really think your father and brother will want you to marry *Paolo*, when you can marry Paris? That's lunacy!"

Caterina sighed. "It isn't as simple as that, Juliet. My father is very anti-nobility. How could you not be, after what my grandfather did to my mother. He loved her, deeply, and she was devastated when her own father left her. Though she's been gone a long time he loves her still and he honours her memory. I have no idea how he will react."

Harriet sat silently, watching the exchange between the two women. The politics of a world she didn't belong in were beyond her – but then, she'd had an effect on Caterina and Juliet already, and their stories were already irrevocably changed. Perhaps if she spoke about what marriage looked like in her time it might give Caterina the courage she needed to face her family.

"Caterina," Harriet said quietly. "I won't pretend to understand how this all works here. It's a world away from my own home. But maybe…would you like to hear how relationships work in the time I am from?"

Caterina nodded, and Juliet swung around to give Harriet her full attention as well.

"We marry for love. Sure, there are people who marry others for money, or fame…sometimes people make mistakes and get divorced." Caterina and Juliet looked shocked.

"Divorced?" Juliet whispered.

"But…that means they'd be excommunicated from the Church!" Caterina exclaimed.

"In my time that's not so important," Harriet said, spreading her hands wide. "Religion isn't as much a part of everyday life as it is in your time. Sure, it means there's more people who are divorced but it also means there are less unhappy marriages."

"What happens to children of those marriages?" Juliet asked, fascinated.

"Yes…well." Harriet considered her own close friends. Some of her best friends came from split homes – two families to spend Christmas with, two families to move between week after week. Some were very happy with the arrangements, others weren't.

"It seems that some people handle it better than others," Harriet said. "I can't speak from personal experience…my parents love each other, even though they fight sometimes. Just about small things, when they're frustrated or angry. But you can tell they love each other. Even when they're snarky, or cranky, there's still a lot of love between them, and they always make up their differences. They chose each other because they fell in love – not because of which part of society they came from, or who they were related to."

Harriet took one hand of each young woman. "I understand it's much more complicated than that in this lifetime. I understand that you don't have the freedom that women have in my time – that comes around in the 1960s I think. But you can start! Surely there are people in your time who marry for love – look at Caterina's parents!" She hurried on as Caterina's face clouded. "I know that your mum died, Cat, and I know it was hard on you, but imagine if she had lived. She would have wanted you to do the same as she did, even if it meant that you had the same life she did. And you *won't*. Paris is offering you his hand in marriage – his power and influence, and if I don't miss my guess, his love as well."

"He certainly never looked at me that way," Juliet teased, with a sidelong glance at her friend. Caterina blushed.

"I have feelings for him too," Caterina admitted, looking away sheepishly. "Paolo will be furious." She sighed. "He will take it out on my brother and father, and their business will suffer."

"But their business will also be protected by Paris and his good name," Juliet exclaimed. "Really, how much damage can Paolo do? People deal with him because they have to, not because they want to. He's the only blacksmith the public of Verona have access to that is any good, even if he is an awful man."

Harriet took both of Caterina's hands and looked her straight in the eye. "If there were no rules, no restrictions, no repercussions to marrying Paris – would you do it?"

"In a heartbeat," Caterina replied steadily.

"Well there you go then!" Harriet said, beaming. "All Juliet and I need to do now is hold you to that." Harriet turned to Juliet. "How long does it take to arrange a marriage in 14th century Verona, Juliet?"

Juliet grinned. "Depends on who you know."

Chapter Fifteen

"And I, Count Paris of Verona, take you, Caterina Margaret Holland, to be my wife." The audience in the little church watched in rapt silence as two of the most glamorous people in Verona pledged their lives to each other. The bride was radiant: gorgeous in her waterfall silk ivory dress. The waist sat low and her sleeves were long, sitting peaked on her shoulders. Caterina's long blonde hair was obscured by the cloud of a white veil that trailed behind her, touching the ground and mingling with the flowing stream of her dress. The golden embroidery on the front of her breathtaking gown shone in the light streaming through the stained glass windows behind the altar.

The groom was also a picture of happiness: his face aglow as he looked at his new bride. He was flanked by a most unlikely pairing – Prince Escalus and Romeo Montague. On Caterina's other side stood Juliet and Harriet, their dresses and styles vastly different in an attempt to conceal the eerie similarities between the two women. Juliet shone in a gown of deep blue while Harriet looked like she really did belong in the 14th century in a borrowed dress of muted gold.

The Sant'Anastasia was full to capacity, and the people who didn't fit in the pews lined the walls flanking the imposing front door. Everyone had wanted to see the nuptials of the popular Paris and his beautiful betrothed, who had seemingly come from nowhere. The pair clearly belonged together, and they were the seemingly uncomplicated love story following on the heels of the spectacular and unexpected Capulet-Montague union.

However, not everyone was happy and their darkness lurked and swirled amongst the joyful crowd. Paolo, the jilted blacksmith, scowled angrily as he turned away from the pulpit and the picture of wedded bliss presented to him. He had taken back the finely crafted saddle he had gifted to Caterina, as expected, but Paris had replaced it with a finer, more intricate one that had once belonged to his mother.

Caterina's brother and father were openly jubilant – in direct contrast to Lady Capulet who stood silently in the front row, pointedly ignoring the Montague contingent in the seats opposite. Alfie beamed at his beautiful sister as Lady Capulet steadily regarded her daughter and new son-in-law standing at the front with their powerful friends. Gone was the image of a giddy woman who obeyed her husband's every order. The frivolous Lady who threw extravagant balls, invited only the most exclusive people and could be as vicious to those in her power as she was weak to those above her.

She was shrouded in black, her veil covering her ravaged face. The events of the last week had taken their toll, physically, and she was too vain to let her face be seen by the people who would have once done extraordinary things to get into her good graces. The resentment burned in her eyes as she regarded the daughter she'd always thought she controlled. Or Capulet controlled, but it was the same thing. The girl she'd raised to obey her father was gone, thrown to the winds as her husband had been.

Capulet sat shackled in the prison of Escalus' castle, waiting for his verdict to be carried out. He was to be excommunicated and banished from Verona, able to be punished by death if he returned. The same indictment he had forced on Romeo Montague.

Alongside him sat Donato, his henchman. But Donato's fate was to be very different. He wasn't highly born and had no wealth to protect him. He was to swing at the end of a hangman's noose for the crime of murder.

Escalus had been waiting for Capulet and his men as they thundered through Verona to the Mantua road. A long line of mounted soldiers, their swords drawn, had faced Capulet as he reigned to a hasty stop. He had been taken into custody and questioned, and the whole sorry story had spilled out. Donato had remained tight lipped to the end – but his master's loyalty had not been so steadfast. Capulet had indeed written a note, but to Donato – not Tybalt. He admitted his role in ordering Donato to steal Tybalt and Romeo's daggers, to kill Mercutio, then Tybalt. He had railed at the injustice of a Montague marrying his only daughter, defiling his family and his good name, while ignoring the hypocrisy of his cold-hearted sacrifice of his protégé.

It had fallen on deaf ears. Escalus had debated his ruling for days, as Caterina and Paris had prepared to marry in a whirlwind courtship. Harriet had agreed to remain long enough to see them wed, seeing as she had come this far, but she was seriously homesick. Besides, it would be difficult to explain to Escalus why

Juliet's cousin would leave Verona as her kinswoman and friend arranged to celebrate their marriages.

Preparing a wedding in 14th century Verona had been surprisingly easy – or at least Harriet supposed it was with the wealth and influence of the ruling family behind them. Friar Lawrence had agreed to conduct the ceremony – who else was there to ask, given his role in their whole saga? Caterina was still adjusting to her rapid change in circumstances, but was secure in the love and regard of her new husband. Paris was truly a man in love – he looked at Caterina in a way that he had never seen Juliet. The two pairs really had ended up with the right person, and it was frightening to think how close they had come to being not one, but two, pairs of doomed lovers.

Alfie Holland was euphorically happy for his sister. His business was now a favourite of royalty; however, it was the breaking of bonds with Paolo that delighted him. He had never truly reconciled marrying his lovely sister to the repugnant blacksmith, but he had also felt the weight of providing for her and ensuring she had a future. He felt that weight lift off now and the happiness shone out of his face. Caterina's father regarded his beautiful daughter with a soft smile. He could see the same look of love on her face that he himself had worn all those years ago. Although his story had been cut short, deep down he wouldn't wish for anything else for his child.

As Caterina and Paris linked arms to walk down the aisle, as man and wife, Romeo and Juliet linked arms behind them. Juliet snuck a small sideways smile at her husband. She, too, would need to adjust to the change in her own circumstances. Lady Juliet Montague had succeeded where others had failed for centuries. She had united the Houses of Montague and Capulet, as had Romeo. But it was Juliet's bravery that had sealed their fate.

As Escalus had debated Capulet's punishment, Juliet had attended Escalus' castle and demanded an audience with her father. Knowing what he had done, she had denounced him. It had hurt her to do so – berating the man who had been her only father figure had been a strange and unusual experience. It was something she might have often wished to do, but would never have dared, just a bare week ago. She was a new Juliet now and she was ready to make some changes.

Escalus was impressed, and he had seen in Juliet, as he did in Caterina, a shift in the way these women were dealing with their stations in life. He was intrigued, and had chosen to break with tradition and confer Capulet's title, wealth and properties onto Juliet. Her mother was also her problem, unless she chose to accompany Capulet into exile, but Escalus did not doubt that Juliet could handle her.

Lord and Lady Montague, Romeo's parents, were shocked to hear their son had married a Capulet. Not as shocked as Juliet's had been, and they hadn't tried to kill anyone to prevent it from happening, but they were still taking their time to adjust to this new situation. It also didn't hurt that the source of the most recent tension was to be banned from Verona forever.

Centuries of bloodshed and in-fighting was now over. This was a major boon for Escalus, as the keeper of peace in Verona, and it was a welcome opportunity for Lord Montague as well. His first act of proving his peaceful intentions was to appoint Alfie and Carlos as his official importers. Their fledgling shipping company finally had some sorely needed financial backing and they would be sailing with their first import shipment in the next few months. They also now had access to the private Montague blacksmith, so Paolo was no longer a problem for them. Alfie could thumb his nose at him all he wanted, and regularly did.

Verona was certainly a different place than it had been a week ago. As Harriet placed her hand on Prince Escalus' arm for their return trip down the aisle, she pondered the impact she'd had on a time and place that wasn't her own. But it had impacted on her too. She understood what it was like – truly understood – to not have a choice, or to feel like you didn't. She still couldn't fathom what life was like for people who lived in poverty and didn't get pulled out of it, like Caterina had been, but she had a better understanding of the politics of the time. And of how to smash through those barriers and make things happen.

Women in this time weren't the meek, submissive beings they were portrayed as in history books. But neither were they as enlightened as women of her own time. There was a spectrum, and Harriet was at the end that was still forging its way into a new time. It would be interesting to see if Juliet and Caterina did anything that would change things for women here and now. Harriet suspected that they would. She smiled at the well-wishers as they threw rice over Caterina and Paris. They emerged out into the mid-morning sunshine to see the piazza and the streets of Verona lined with people from all walks of life. It seemed everyone in the city had turned out to watch the happy couple marry. A series of carriages waited at the bottom of the steps of the Sant'Anastasia, charged with conveying their party to the Capulet Manor for the wedding banquet. It was to be a double celebration of the marriages of two wonderful women.

Juliet and Harriet carefully bundled Caterina into the first carriage, Paris holding his new wife's hand and seating her with an elegant flourish. The long silken train and veil folded into the carriage, they closed the door and Paris and Caterina waved to the crowds as they went slowly through the streets. Romeo, Juliet, Harriet and Escalus settled into the second carriage.

Escalus sighed and leaned back in his seat, closing his eyes briefly.

"It's been a long week," he said, his voice low and gravelly. He opened his eyes and regarded Harriet intently, seated across from him. He stared a moment longer, then closed his eyes again. "No, I'm still not going to ask. I don't want to know the answer." Escalus knew there was something off about Harriet's appearance in Verona, but he was too smart to ask for more details.

Harriet snuck a smile at Juliet, who squeezed her hand in response. It was getting closer to the moment when they were going to try to get Harriet back to her own time, and she was getting more and more nervous as it approached.

"Probably wise," Romeo said with a grin. Escalus made a noise that sounded suspiciously like a grunt.

"My Lord," Juliet said, leaning forward earnestly. "I do want to thank you. I don't think that I've really had a proper chance in the lead up to the wedding. What you did for me – for us – was unprecedented. I know that tradition and custom says that my father's estate should have passed to Romeo as my husband, but thank you for passing it into my care. It shows that you have faith in me, and I will do my utmost to honour that."

With Escalus' decision, Juliet had become one of the first women to hold a title in her own right, not just through marriage to her husband. It was a step that might seem to be limited now, but Harriet knew from her perspective on history that it was steps like these that paved the way for much larger reforms. Juliet had a great appreciation for what Escalus had done and her time with Harriet had encouraged her to show that appreciation, in much the same way a man would do. Juliet herself knew that she had changed – she was stronger somehow – than before Harriet had come into her life. She was also alive, and given Harriet's knowledge of the Shakespearean play, perhaps she might not be if Harriet had not come through that time portal of hers. She was grateful for her new friend, while at the same time knowing she had to let her go back to her own family.

The two women in the carriage remained lost in their thoughts while Romeo and Escalus conversed quietly in the darkened interior. It was but a short ride to Capulet Manor – now Romeo and Juliet's home – and they had arrived in good time.

Juliet and Harriet were handed out of the carriage and hurried over to help Caterina alight from hers. They need not have bothered, and they watched as Paris gripped his wife lightly around the waist and lifted her down, setting her on the ground as if she weighed nothing. Caterina's cheeks were stained a delicate pink and her brilliant blue eyes were sparkling with happiness. She looked alive in a way that she hadn't a mere week ago, and she was a picture of lovely contentment.

The little group swept up the front steps of Capulet Manor and into the front hall. The grand staircase stood imposingly in front of them and they climbed to the first landing. The ladies had to go to the left, the men to the right, to refresh before the guests arrived and the married couples were introduced.

"This is where I first saw you," Romeo said with a wistful smile for his wife. "You were standing right here, in this spot. You were so beautiful, I felt like I couldn't breathe. I had to know who you were, and when I found out…well. That was complicated, but our story is like no other and I wouldn't change it for the world."

Juliet smiled at her husband. She took his hand and squeezed it. "I wouldn't either," she replied quietly. "Now, anyway!"

Paris and Romeo knew that the women were intending to try and send Harriet back before the wedding banquet. Two women in the same room for that length of time who looked so alike as Juliet and Harriet did would raise questions, and Harriet was anxious to return to her own family.

Paris was the first to address Harriet. He took one of her hands, raised it to his lips and kissed it gallantly. "Thank you," he said.

"For drugging you?" Harriet replied, a twinkle in her eye. Paris laughed, but then sobered. "Actually, yes. If you hadn't, who knows how our lives would have played out. If I hadn't met Cat…well. I never would have known true happiness. For that I cannot thank you enough." Paris bowed and stepped back. Romeo took his place. He grinned and folded Harriet in a bear hug, as one of her brothers might have done.

"Thanks for saving my hide, Harriet," he whispered in her ear before he released her. "Thank you for my wife, and for our story." He stepped back and took Juliet's hand, raising it to his lips. She smiled radiantly and he let it go reluctantly.

"Good luck," Romeo said, and he and Paris turned to follow Escalus into their wing of the manor.

"Come on," Caterina said, a twinkle in her eye as she stood on the top step, near to the next landing. Her gorgeous dress cascaded down the steps behind her. "We have a pretty extraordinary young woman to send home."

The three walked, arms linked, into Juliet's old room. It was where Harriet had arrived and they believed it would be a fitting place for her to leave. Harriet looked around at the stone walls, the tapestries and the massive four poster bed.

She looked back at her new friends. They were watching her intently.

"You know, if it doesn't work," Juliet said, sensing Harriet's nerves. "There's no reason why you can't stay here!"

Harriet smiled. "As much as I appreciate that, I sort of miss my brothers. More than I thought I would, that's for sure! And I miss my parents, so much."

"Harriet, you've changed us. You've changed our stories. Is there anything we can do to thank you?" Caterina regarded her new friend sadly, knowing she had to go but not wanting to be parted.

Harriet choked back a sadness she hadn't thought would be there. "You're both very special women. You have a role to play here, and I can't tell you what that is. All I can say is to be brave, be strong and do what you think is right. I can't pretend to understand what it's like to live here all the time, day after day, year after year. But I want to go back and read something about you in the history books – or about any woman in this time for that matter. Even if you write it yourself, or someone else does. Do something that lets future generations know what it's like for you. That's what you can do for me."

"You know," Caterina said ponderously. "I think we can manage that?" She looked at Juliet. Juliet nodded.

Harriet reached into the folds of her sleeves and pulled out the crumpled paper that she hadn't been without since she'd arrived in this time. She unfolded it and smoothed it out, studying the lines of the face she had created with her own hand. She looked up at her friends.

"So…what do I do?" Harriet's fingers nervously smoothed the wrinkles in the paper. "Well," Juliet said, frowning. "You said that you came through when you were asleep and you woke up here. You said that the page ended up next to you somehow."

"Yes, it was next to my face when I woke up," Harriet said.

"Maybe if you look at it and concentrate on it?" Caterina suggested. Harriet held the paper up to her face and stared at it, the lines of graphite swimming on the paper in front of her. She lowered the paper in frustration. "Nothing's happening. If it were that easy, I'd have been back home already!"

Juliet smiled. "You must be patient, Harriet," she said. "I imagine these things don't happen easily."

"These things aren't supposed to happen at all," Harriet said, a touch tersely. She was anxious to get back home, anxious that it wouldn't work. Caterina touched her arm soothingly.

"It's okay, Harriet," she said. "Juliet and I are here. And if we can't solve it now, we will." Impulsively, Caterina leant over and hugged Harriet tightly. "I'm so glad to have met you," she whispered. Juliet embraced both women and they stood there, a trio interlocked. The paper rustled between them as they united.

A bright flash lit up the dim room and Harriet began to glow. She looked at her arms, then at Juliet and Caterina, her eyes wide. Both ladies released her and stood back, watching as Harriet turned golden, sparkling in the semi darkness like a diamond winking in the wall of a mine. Slowly, Harriet began to fade from sight, the drawing clutched in her hand. She waved at her friends, smiling a little sadly as she watched them fade away.

With a sudden snap, Harriet was gone and the paper she'd been holding fluttered to the floor. Caterina hurried over to pick it up. She turned and held it out to Juliet.

"I think this belongs with you, my friend," she said, folding Juliet's hand over the paper. Juliet smiled and put her other hand over Caterina's. It certainly did.

Chapter Sixteen

Harriet blinked in the morning sunlight of her own room. The white curtains billowed in the breeze as the fresh morning air rushed through the windows. The light reflected off the pool below her window and danced on the ceiling: tiny rainbows chasing each other over the white roof.

Disoriented, she half sat up and looked around her room. Everything was in place – just as it should have been. She was wearing the clothes she had fallen asleep in, after the argument with her mother, and her books were all over the desk, just as they had been before she went to sleep.

As she shifted in the bed, Harriet heard the rustle of paper. She looked down to see the face she had drawn staring back at her – so like her own but subtly different. She knew in that moment that it hadn't all been a dream. She didn't understand it – not yet – but she knew, just as she knew that she was now home, that it had all been real.

Harriet slid out of bed and carefully placed the drawing on the top shelf of her desk. She raced to the door and threw it open. It was still early, and the house lay relatively silent. But Harriet didn't care. She bounded to Mason's room and flung his door open. There he was, his messy head sticking out from under the covers. It didn't matter how hot it was, Mason could always be found under his blankets. But always with one foot sticking out. Harriet walked over and placed a kiss on his head. She'd missed her little brother, though she'd deny it if ever pressed on it. Mason murmured in his sleep and flipped over to face the window. His light snore indicated he'd gone straight back to sleep. Harriet grinned and darted out of his room.

She hurried down the hallway to Tristan's room. She pitched the door open with such force that it sprang back against the door stopper.

"Hey!" Tristan yelped in surprise as he yanked his t-shirt on. He swung to face the door and his sister, framed in its opening. Harriet sprang in, kissed him on the cheek and bounced back out again. Tristan stared after her, then shrugged and turned back to his bed, throwing the covers up in an attempt to make it look like he'd made it.

Harriet hurried down the stairs.

"Mum, Dad!" she said as she skidded to a halt at the bottom.

"Where's the fire, kiddo?" Logan Hunter asked from his seat at the table. He was finishing his coffee and the morning paper. Harriet dropped a kiss on his head as she walked past. He looked mildly surprised but returned to the sports section readily enough.

"You're up early!" Carolyn Hunter turned from the stove where she'd been finishing off some scrambled eggs that smelled slightly burned. She squeaked in surprise as her daughter barrelled up to her and threw her arms around her waist.

"This is nice. What's this for?" Carolyn asked, her voice slightly strangled as Harriet squeezed tight.

"Just because," Harriet said, easing off a little. She snatched some eggs from her mother's plate and grinned as Carolyn sent a half-hearted, poorly aimed smack at her hand.

"You have that English assignment due on Monday," Carolyn reminded Harriet as she took out another plate for her daughter and ladled eggs onto it.

"Hmm mm," Harriet said as she bit into her first mouthful of eggs. She closed her eyes in bliss. There was nothing quite like a home cooked meal, even if it was a little charred. Especially if you knew it wouldn't kill you.

"It says you have to rewrite Romeo and Juliet with a different ending," Carolyn continued as she bustled around the kitchen. She missed the twinkle that came into her daughter's eye. "Do you have any ideas on what you might do?"

"Oh," Harriet said, confidence clear in her voice. "I've got this one in the bag." She grinned a little to herself. Logan raised an eyebrow across the table at his daughter, then smiled at his wife.

"I was thinking, if you've finished it before this afternoon we could have a camp out in the backyard tonight, have a fire, live a little rough?"

Harriet smiled. She'd done enough rough living for the time being. "I'll be sleeping in my own bed, thank you! But I'd love a fire pit Dad, and some roasted marshmallows. I don't think it'll take me long to do, get your firewood ready."

Harriet scraped the last of her eggs off her plate and rose from the table. She put her plate into the dishwasher and wiped her hands. It was time to get this story out there.

***

A few hours later, Harriet leant back in her desk chair and stretched her back. She flexed her fingers and studied the papers in front of her. The story was all there, in black and white. This time though, it was told in Juliet's voice – through her eyes. At the end stood two pairs of lovers, deeply content that they had found the right person in an age where marrying for love wasn't often a priority. Harriet was particularly proud of the way she had captured Juliet – the real Juliet. She had always been a firecracker – Harriet had known that the moment she met her at the cabin in the woods. But now, with her father out of the way and some powerful friends, she was a force to be reckoned with. She was an example to women and young girls, rather than just a victim in her own story. And Caterina. She hadn't even been in the original story and Harriet had to wonder if that was because she just wouldn't have allowed the tragedy to unfold. Cat was a strong, courageous woman and she was only going to become more influential with her marriage to Paris.

Harriet sat back and thought of Juliet and Caterina. How she would have loved to see them in this day and age. Would they have adjusted, as she had, to their version of normal? Would they have found their way through a world that was completely foreign to them? She tended to think they would have. Though there were differences between the three young women, there were also remarkable similarities. Resilience, flexibility, trust, faith and intelligence. It was all there, crossing centuries, cultures and civilisations.

Harriet intended to visit the library on Monday morning. She wanted to look at texts about medieval women and study in a little more depth what had been written about them. Or more accurately – what had not. There had to be other stories just like Juliet's…ones where the characters had to be more than just the victims of other people's decisions.

Harriet shook her head abruptly. She'd only just returned to her own time: she certainly didn't want to entertain thoughts of entering another just yet.

Satisfied with her story, Harriet gathered her papers and sought out the rest of her family. She found them sitting around the fire pit outside, the sparks from the blaze flying high into the twilight sky. Her father handed her a perfectly melted marshmallow as she sat down. Handing her paper to her mother, Harriet devoured her first marshmallow. She polished off another five before she was done, much to her grumbling brothers' displeasure. Across the fire, Carolyn's eyes met Harriet's as she finished reading her re-telling of Romeo and Juliet. She nodded, a slight smile on her face. Harriet leant back in her chair, satisfied and content in her mother's approval. As she stared into the flames, Harriet reflected on the radical changes to Romeo and Juliet's tale. The makings of a different story had all been there. They just needed an outsider, someone different, to give them a push.

If only all tragedies had someone to help them reach their happily ever after.

Into the Abyss is the first novel by young adult author, Marissa Price.

Loved the story?

Harriet's tale continues in the next book: *Into the Abyss: Scourge of Scotland*, coming to The Literature Factory publishing division in February 2018!

9 780648 127901